MW00899367

Goodness Falls

Scott.

Thanks for your support, and continuing friendship! I have great admiration for your dedication & contributions as a coach and educator. I hope you enjoy GF!

All the Best,

6/7/14

First Edition Design Publishing

Goodness Falls
Copyright ©2014 Ty Roth

ISBN 978-1622-875-29-0 PRINT
ISBN 978-1622-875-30-6 PRINT HC
ISBN 978-1622-875-28-3 EBOOK

LCCN 2014932032

May 2014

Published and Distributed by
First Edition Design Publishing, Inc.
P.O. Box 20217, Sarasota, FL 34276-3217
www.firsteditiondesignpublishing.com

"I have come to disappoint you."

from "When Goodness Falls" by
Northern Portrait

Goodness Falls

a novel by ty roth

Prologue

"A tragedy starts high and ends low," Mr. Mortis, subbing in senior English for Mr. Miller, lectured on that October Friday, whose night would begin the unfolding of events that have left me in this place writing this journal in the tiniest of print inside a pocket-sized notebook and trying to piece together the shard-like memories of those events.

Dr. Young encourages me to write or draw or paint but only under supervised conditions and with the understanding that, whatever I do write, draw, or paint, it will be collected and analyzed. So I'm forced to write late at night or in the early morning in starts and stops in the semi-darkness of my room and in-between regular peek-ins by third shift staff. During the day, I tape the notebook to the bottom of my mattress, and I stuff it inside my underwear whenever I leave the room, which is awkward because they only allow me boxers. They search the room but not my underwear – at least not while I'm wearing it. I know they search my room because, sometimes, when I return from counseling, or a meal, or social hour, something's not quite right: like my toothbrush is turned; or my miniature, football-shaped, polyurethane stress ball is slightly off kilter on its tiny holder; or my folded t-shirts are slightly rumpled inside the dresser. I'm not OCD. I'm careful. There's a difference.

The notebook is my back-up memory, an external hard drive of sorts. I need it because every day my brain is growing more addled by the painkillers, the antidepressants, and the antipsychotic drugs I'm fed to combat what Dr. Young calls my PMD, or Psychotic Major Depression. Psychotic. Can you believe that? Crazy. Isn't it? Dr. Young says I have delusional, hallucinatory, and paranoid tendencies. But I know what I saw, and no one's going to convince me differently – even if it does sound . . . well . . . delusional, hallucinatory, and paranoid.

I'm told that I'm also a bit of a celebrity for being one of the youngest patients ever diagnosed with Chronic Traumatic Encephalopathy (CTE). It's what they used to call "punch drunk" when referring to boxers who'd taken too many fists to the head. It's a degenerative brain disease that acts like Alzheimer's, except I just turned eighteen. Dr. Young tells me I'm a hot property in the medical and football communities because, until very recently, CTE was only discoverable through a microscope trained on dissected brain tissue – from a corpse.

Dr. Young says I'm lucky to be alive.

Whatever.

Chapter One

Friday, October 26, 201_

"Tragedies start high . . ."

"It's too easy," I thought as I surveyed the defense and stole a peek at the clock ticking off the game's final seconds.

The roar of the crowd neared jet-engine decibels through the ear holes in my battle-scarred helmet. Down by five in the last game of the season, our spot in the playoffs rested on the outcome of that final play, yet I felt calm and confident. Unlike pretty much everything else in life, football made sense to me. For some kids, it's math or hip-hop or engines. For me, it had always been football. Since I was just a little kid playing pee wee ball, it was on the football field and during the manic eight seconds of an average play that I felt most comfortable and the most alive. Eight seconds a play multiplied by approximately sixty offensive plays a game over a ten-game season equaled eighty minutes of high-quality living a year. That doesn't amount to much, but I bet it's more than most people get. And if we scored on that final play, the game, the season, my life would be extended for at least another eight minutes into the playoffs.

In the shotgun formation with my knees slightly bent and my hands flashing palms towards the big butt of my best friend and center, David Mooseburger, I lifted my foot to signal the left slot back into motion. I watched him cross in front of me and draw the Greene County defensive back to the other side of the formation.

Greene County's inside linebacker walked out wide, replaced the re-positioned defensive back, and tipped off his intention to blitz from the back side. Coach Harris had called for, and I had signaled to my teammates, a screen pass to Cory Morrison, the tailback. But I had no intention of throwing the ball.

On "Hut!" Moose's snap spiraled towards me. The upraised strings on the ball's cowhide surface made three revolutions during its flight into my hands. Like at the snap of a hypnotist's fingers, I slipped into a hyper-sensitive state. The universe contracted and time morphed into slow motion.

"Where ya going?!" Morrison screamed, as I improvised a quarterback draw play, which advertised itself as a pass but was actually a run.

I could feel the backside linebacker barreling down on me, but I calmly held the ball cocked in a pass ready position under my chin and directed my eyes toward my receivers. I stood statuesquely inside the fast-collapsing pocket and waited until the skeptical front side linebacker finally bought the pass, abandoned the line of scrimmage, sprinted into his pass drop, and opened a running lane. At the last possible moment, I dipped my shoulders and sent the backside blitzer flying over the top of me with a desperate clutch at my black jersey with a green number six.

Stepping forward, I avoided the attacking defensive linemen, and with the linebackers removed by blitz or pass drop and the defensive backs chasing decoy receivers, I scrambled toward the end zone. At the three yard line, I dove like Superman and stretched all of my six feet, two inch frame and the ball toward the goal line.

A referee's whistle signaled the touchdown while I was still airborne.

The game was over.

We had won!

I had lived to live another eighty minutes!

But out of nowhere, a frustrated Greene County defender ear holed me, driving the crown of his helmet into my left temple. A black curtain descended over my consciousness, and I dropped like a rag doll onto the rock-hard field turf.

I surfaced from the blackness with the crushing weight of my dog-piling teammates pressing me into the earth. I couldn't breathe.

Asphyxiation!

But soon the weight of the near-ton of teammates' bodies in their sweat-drenched skin and uniforms relented and re-admitted a trickling flow of oxygen into my death-reprieved lungs, and the momentarily knocked-offline neurons in my brain commenced the slow process of rebooting.

I was shocked that it was Morrison who offered his hand and pulled me to my unsteady feet; however, he remained true to form. "That should have been my touchdown, asshole," he spit through his mouth guard and walked away.

Clearing my vision and gathering my bearings and my marbles amid the mass of teammates and the fans who had rushed the field, I spied the bodies of several Greene County players sprawled flat with face masks and fists pressed heavily into the turf. A part of me felt sorry for them but only a small part. Mostly, I was glad to still be alive and headed for the playoffs.

Moose grabbed me from behind, gave me a rib-crunching bear hug, and lifted me clean off my feet before returning me to the ground. None of which helped my disorientation. "Dude, look at your helmet! I ain't never seen that before," he slurred through his mouthpiece and pink cheeks, pinched together into a blowfish-face inside his helmet.

"What?" I asked to buy time for the fog inside my head to clear.

Moose ripped off his helmet by the facemask. "I said your helmet is trashed."

I slipped off my state-of-the art, supposedly concussion-proof helmet over my longish, black curls and held it up for inspection. A hairline fracture zigzagged across its hard plastic shell like a bolt of lightning from the dome of the helmet down toward the left ear hole.

"Coach is going to be pissed," Moose said. Coach Harris regularly reminded us that each helmet drained upwards of four hundred dollars from his football budget, and mine cost nearly twice that. "Screw him, dude," Moose added on second thought. "We're in the playoffs. *Carpe Diem*, motherfucker!"

Carpe Diem, "Seize the Day," had been the theme for the readings in our first unit in Mr. Miller's English class. Moose and I had immediately adopted it as the motto for our senior football season. Before each game, we inscribed it in black Sharpie on the white athletic tape we wore over our wrists. "Carpe Diem," I repeated.

Moose let loose a war whoop and joined our teammates and the mass of Fighting Ducks fans who had swarmed the field in celebratory bedlam. The Goodness Falls sports teams were nicknamed for the insane number and the wide variety of ducks that frequented the creeks, ponds, and lakes in the area. Like the damn ducks during migratory seasons, the Ducks' fans were everywhere. One girl, dressed in all black and whom I didn't even recognize, ran in out of nowhere, jumped up into Moose's arms, and gave him an open-mouthed kiss. Moose's shocked yet blissful expression was priceless. I couldn't help but smile. Having been best friends for nearly our entire lives, I'm pretty sure it was his first girl kiss – and last. I laughed, turned away, and began weaving a wobbly-kneed course through a mass of back-slapping well-wishers until I was violently horse-collared from behind by an irate Coach Harris.

"Just what do you think you were doing, Farrell?"

"Sir?"

If you can't run the plays I call, I'll play a quarterback who will!"

I held my helmet by the face mask and hid it behind my back. "Coach . . ." I tried to respond with a lucid explanation, but the words proved as elusive as butterflies inside my still-scattered brain. It didn't matter. He wasn't interested in what I had to say anyway.

"Maybe you think that I won't sit your ass down. Well, let me tell you, son, Terwilliger has looked pretty sharp running the second team. He's hungry for an opportunity. He'll run what I call and not pull a stunt like you just did. You're just one piss-me-off away from me pulling the trigger."

"But, Coach," I slurred. "I scored. We won."

"I don't give a damn that you scored or we won." Purplish veins popped in his neck. "You run what *I* call! You *never* show me up!"

"Yes, sir," was all I could muster.

Coach Harris maintained his steely-eyed gaze for what seemed like forever. "Christ, Farrell, your pupils look like the goddamned Holland Tunnel. Stay away from Schultzie. That mothering son-of-a-bitch will want to bench you for sure if he gets one good look at you."

Schultzie was the athletic trainer. Coach Harris didn't much care for trainers telling him who could or couldn't play. He preferred his own old school remedies to injuries usually involving "rubbing some dirt on it," "shaking it off," or "sucking it up." He had little-to-no-use for the coddling methods of modern sports medicine.

More or less inured to Coach's temper tantrums but still frightened to cross him, I shrugged off his tirade and searched the sidelines for my girlfriend. Caly was what you might call a throwback like the old-time jerseys NFL teams sometimes wear. She was a straight-edged honor student and an unapologetic member of the cheerleading squad even if it left her on the wrong side of the much cooler, snarky girls at school. She believed equally in school spirit and the holy spirit without skepticism or irony.

I spied Caly with her blond hair pulled back tightly into a pony tail and her cheeks stained crimson by the cold. She waited inside her lined, cold weather track suit behind the emptied Ducks' bench with her pom-pom hidden hands pressed tightly to her breasts.

"Nice pom-poms," I teased, concentrating hard on my pronunciation and trying not to betray my wooziness.

"You're looking kind of sexy yourself in those tight football pants," Caly teased while rising onto her tiptoes and throwing her arms around my neck. "Do you have it?" She asked and smiled expectantly.

I released her, backed up a step, reached deep inside the collar of my jersey behind the breastplate of my shoulder pads, and slowly hauled up a chain on the end of which hung Caly's tiny, gold class ring with a garnet stone.

Her face lit up.

"You?" I asked.

She partially unzipped her jacket, reached inside the white turtle neck she wore beneath her green cheerleading top, and pulled out my larger but otherwise matching class ring. "Always?" She asked.

"And forever," I answered. "Meet me?"

She answered in the affirmative by returning to her tiptoes and kissing me on my chapped lips. "Oh, gross!"

"You know you love it," I said, keeping my words monosyllabic, then jogged off to the locker room.

*****

Lingering inside a slow-to-dissipate brain fog, I sat on the bench in front of my locker and stared at my shoelaces rather than celebrating the victory with my teammates. Moose managed to steal me four extra-strength aspirin from Schultzie's trainer's kit to combat my intensifying headache. Eventually, I showered and faced the cheerless custom of a post-game meeting with my parents outside the Ducks' locker room. By which time and despite the aspirin, the once gently tinkling sleigh bells inside my head had given way to massive gong strikes.

Beneath his brown Carhartt jacket, my dad wore his everyday work overalls and work boots; although, he hadn't worked since the meatpacking plant closed fifteen years earlier. My mom wore her green "My Son's the Quarterback" sweatshirt with my number and "Farrell" on the back, a pair of stonewashed mom jeans, and a pair of those navy blue and tan duck boots that haven't been in style since she was in high school.

"Great game, T.J.!" My mom squealed at a pitch that penetrated my skull like one of those ultrasonic weapons riot police use to disperse unruly mobs.

I winced.

"We are so proud of you!" As usual my mom spoke loudly enough for everyone nearby to hear and to thrust me into an unwanted spotlight, unwanted by me at least.

Everyone nearby suddenly felt obligated to throw in their "Attaboys" and "Great Game, T.J.s"

It was humiliating.

"Thanks, Mom. Can we not talk so loud?"

"Nonsense. You're the hero," she said at a frequency just below dog whistle.

"It's a team game. I'm not the hero," I tried to explain, but her attention had already been drawn over my shoulder.

She suddenly sang, "Well, hello, Dr. Stone." Her breath was tinted with the peppermint schnapps she'd mixed into her thermos of hot chocolate.

"Mrs. Farrell, I'd like a quick word with T.J. here," Dr. Stone said while reluctantly condescending to plant a light kiss on my mother's rosy cheek.

Though still within an extended arm's reach, my dad backed away and somehow managed to become invisible, as he always did in the presence of anyone he considered his social superior, which was just about everyone in and around my hometown of Goodness Falls, named for the natural, ten-foot waterfall that Cold Creek carved into the fertile Ohio soil over eons of meandering towards Lake Erie a few miles to the north. Josiah Goodness, an eighteenth century settler who had farmed the acres surrounding the falls, lent his name to the falls and to the village that later sprang up around his homestead. Today the falls cascade into the limestone subsoil, where the creek crosses Main Street and bisects the village at its exact center. They're a favorite destination for local lovers, naturalists, and suicides.

Dr. Stone wrapped his right arm a little too snugly around my neck and pulled me away from my folks. "Great game tonight, T.J."

"Thanks, Dr. Stone. My teammates really . . ."

"Yeah, yeah, your teammates. I didn't wait all this time to talk about your teammates."

"Yes, sir."

"I'm not going to lie to you, T.J., and I don't think what I'm about to say will come as any kind of surprise."

Past Dr. Stone's shoulder, I could see my mom smiling ear-to-ear at the sight of her boy hobnobbing, as she would call it, with a member of Goodness Falls' gentry.

"My daughter cares deeply for you, and despite my best efforts, it doesn't appear that's going to change anytime soon."

"Yes, sir. I hope not, sir."

"The problem is that Caly is going to college next fall at the University of Toledo, and after graduation, she'll attend the medical college there, where, as you know, I'm on staff."

"That's what she tells me."

"Her biology major will require her total focus, which is going to be difficult if she's mooning over a boyfriend back home."

"Yes, sir," I said for the lack of a better response and hoping to keep the conversation as brief as possible.

"I could simply forbid the relationship, but you know Caly. If I were to do that, she would continue to see you if only to spite me."

"I hope it would be for better reasons than that, sir."

Dr. Stone shot me a glance that communicated his expectation of zero rebuttal, which was fine because the pain in my head was making it increasingly difficult to concentrate on his words or to form my own. "Should you two manage to stay together throughout your senior year and next summer, I can't risk sending Caly off to college with her mind in Toledo but her heart back home in Goodness Falls. She's not strong that way. Do you understand?"

"Yes, sir. I do." Even if it was correct, I resented his assumption that I would still be 'back home in Goodness Falls' and that I couldn't afford to go off to college myself. I'd been offered some partial football scholarships from several division two schools and all sorts of grant-in-aid packages from division three colleges, but none were sufficient enough to meet my financial need.

"I don't think you do."

"Sir?"

"As crazy as this sounds, I'm going to need you in Toledo for as long as Caly needs you in Toledo. It's not the ideal situation. Trust me. And if and when you two break up, Caly's mother and I won't shed any tears. However, I'm a practical man, T.J., a doer. I didn't get to where I am by standing back or by sticking my head in the sand. If you and Caly are going to be together, we need to work on making you into a suitable, potential [He placed extra emphasis on potential.] husband and, [He seemed to choke a little on the still-forming words.] son-in-law."

I loved Caly, but at eighteen the notion of marriage or having Dr. Stone for a father-in-law made me a little uncomfortable. "Yes, sir."

"So here's what we're going to do. I have contacts in the athletic department at the university. My old college roommate is now the athletic director. He tells me that the football team has a handful of scholarships still available for next season. Apparently, several of next year's recruits have uncommitted."

"I spoke with them last spring, but they said all they could offer was a spot as a walk-on, but my family can't . . ."

"You're not listening. I said I have contacts and there are new scholarship opportunities available. T.J.? T.J.! Are you paying attention?"

"Yes, sir," I answered through a wince precipitated by the sudden tightening of the vise squeezing my skull which had temporarily stolen my focus. "You have contacts."

"Tomorrow morning, say seven o'clock, I'm going to pick you up right here, and you and I are going to make a visit to campus, attend the Rockets' game, tour the facilities, and meet with the coaching staff."

"Yes, sir," I said, "but Moose and me have plans to go duck hunting tomorrow."

"Cancel them. I assume you have access to some kind of highlight tape, disc, or something."

"Yes, sir. It has last year's games and the first nine of this season."

"That'll be fine. Seven o'clock sharp."

"Yes, sir. I'll be ready."

The talk was over. Dr. Stone softened his expression, turned his attention to my parents, and made a slight wave. "You all enjoy the rest of your weekend. I'll see *you* in the morning, T.J."

"What'd he say?" My mom asked, sounding like a schoolgirl.

"Dr. Stone's taking me to Toledo tomorrow on a recruiting visit. He said he may be able to hook me up with a scholarship."

"I told you something good was coming!" My mom screeched. "I've been praying on it. I've been praying for a miracle and this is it!" She threw her arms around my waist, squeezed, and planted her cheek against my sternum.

I wanted to dig a hole and bury myself.

"Mom. Mom. There's no guarantee. It's just a visit," I said, but inside, I was thrilled over the potential opportunity to extend my football life, education, and time with Caly.

My mom, however, was having none of my low keying of the situation. In her mind, God had already made up his, and her boy was going to college. She wrapped her sausage fingers around the back of my neck, pulled my face down, and kissed me on the lips.

"Mom, that's enough. Everyone's watching!"

"Let them watch!" She said loudly. "My boy is going to college." She finally loosened her submission hold but kept her fleshy arms wrapped around my midsection and embarrassing me. "Did you hear that, Thomas Joseph?" She turned and said to my dad in the annoying way she had of using both of our first and middle names when excited or angry. "T.J.'s going to college."

My dad grunted something then turned and walked toward his battered and rusted 1992 Ford Ranger pickup with the extended cab.

"Okay, Mom. I didn't say that. I said it was a visit." I literally reached around my back and peeled her hands from off of me. "I have to go. Caly's waiting for me." She'd been standing out of earshot with a group of other cheerleaders who were waiting for their Ducks boyfriends. I waved over my mom's head to Caly. She gave me the WTF palms up, shoulder shrug.

I was apologizing even before I reached her. "I, uh, I couldn't get the truck. My dad, he and my mom, uh, they're, uh . . ."

"It's not a problem," she said, sweetly pretending it was the first time rather than the hundredth that I'd been left without a vehicle and reliant upon her to drive. "My parents left me the Escalade."

The cool of the evening had finally penetrated my layers of a thermal, long-sleeved undershirt; a plaid flannel button down; an unzipped, cotton hoodie; and holey-kneed blue jeans. The only things still warm on me were my feet inside their untied, knock-off Timberland boots. I slung my mesh equipment bag over my shoulder and took Caly by the hand. We walked over the stone parking lot to where the brand new, totally-loaded, totally-sick, ice-black metallic Escalade was parked.

"Daddy says its mine to keep the day you and I break up," she taunted me and pressed a button on the key fob. The headlights flashed and the door locks clicked open.

"My dad says the same thing about his Ranger," I teased.

"That's not funny," Caly said, apparently genuinely hurt by my suggestion of even the possibility of my breaking up with her.

"Oh, I see." I stopped, set my bag on the stones, reached inside her track suit jacket, and tickled her ribs. "Daddy's little girl can dish it out, but she can't take it."

Caly laughed, contorted herself, and twisted away from me. "Stop it. It's not funny when *you* say it. There's not a girl in this town over the age of twelve or under twenty-one who wouldn't jump your bones in a second if we ever broke up. I swear. Sometimes I wonder why you stay with me. I'm far from the prettiest girl in Goodness Fall."

"You don't put out either," I added. For which I received a slap on the shoulder. "Careful!" I said with mock concern. "That's my throwing arm."

"T.J., I'm serious."

"No you're not. You're fishing for compliments. Now I'm supposed to tell you how hot you are." I sidled up close once more and slipped my hands back inside Caly's jacket, where I clasped them together pressed against the small of her back and pulled her in close. "You'll blush. Those adorable dimples will appear, and then you'll cuddle up all nice and close like this."

"Then what?" She said already softening and warming to my predictions.

"Then we'll drive the Escalade to some dead end road in Resthaven, where we'll make out until our tongues swell and our jaws ache."

"And?"

"Then you'll drop me off at Moose's to hang out with the guys and so you don't miss your midnight curfew."

"And that's enough?"

"And that's enough. For now. Besides, tonight *I* got a headache."

"Did you get hit in the head again?" She asked with genuine concern.

"It's nothing."

When we reached the Escalade, I ducked as quickly as I could into what the guys called the "bitch" seat whenever the girl was driving, the shotgun seat otherwise. I slouched as low as possible. Caly all but skipped around to the driver's side and climbed in behind the leather steering wheel.

"When are you going to let me drive you home and come in to meet your parents?" She asked.

"That would be never."

"We'll see about that. You know I love you, T.J. Farrell, even if you are too ashamed of me to introduce me to your parents."

"Yeah, right. My mom thinks you're Miss America and Mother Teresa all rolled up into one, and I love you too, Dr. Caly Stone."

"Someday it'll be Dr. Caly Stone-*Farrell*," she said wistfully, glancing at me sideways, "and I won't have to drop you off, and you won't have a headache, and we won't have to stop at kissing."

I'm not sure if the weird buzzing in my head was from imagining Caly's vision of our futures or from my intensifying headache, but I tried to keep the mood playful. "You too? What's with all the marriage talk tonight?"

"So Daddy did talk to you!" Caly squawked and turned fully towards me with her eyes wide and earnest. "Why didn't you say so? Isn't it the best news? You can keep playing football and we can stay together!"

I tried not to look too sappy. I mean, what would the guys think? But I wanted her to know that I didn't exactly hate the idea. I couldn't stop the stupid grin from spreading across my face. "It is great," I said and meant it.

We drove out of the stadium parking lot, into the blink-and-you'll-miss-it downtown, over Cold Creek, past the falls, and towards the Resthaven Nature Preserve. But as soon as Caly turned onto Oxbo Road, I pleaded with her to pull over. I scrambled out of the Escalade, fell to my hands and knees, and vomited several ounces of fruit punch Gatorade onto the gravel in the middle of the road.

Caly hurried to my side, rubbed my back through my final wretches, then handed me a half-empty bottle of water.

"Maybe you should take me home," I said.

"Just rinse your mouth out real good, and we can still make out."

"Really?"

"No! I was kidding."

"Oh. You know I would have."

"Gross!"

10

Chapter Two

Saturday, October 27, 201_

I'd been named the starting quarterback part way into my junior season. Coach Harris inserted me into the line-up to replace an ineffective senior, who had been leading the Ducks to a shockingly mediocre record. My promotion was largely due to the pressure placed upon Coach by members of the football boosters, led by its president, Dr. Stone. The change resulted in a seven game win streak deep into the state playoffs. Ironically, it probably saved Coach's job.

The senior quarterback I replaced was Donny Harris, Coach's son. Donny never played another down of football. I'd sometimes still see him around, hanging with a bunch of stoners. Coach, at least partially and completely irrationally, blamed me for stealing what was supposed to be Donny's success, and he never forgave the boosters, himself, or me for that substitution.

*****

My mom woke me to drive me to the stadium. The pain in my head had been dialed down to a dull ache. "Wear your church clothes. First impressions are lasting impressions," she insisted.

I could only imagine the impression I'd be making on the other recruits, most of whom would be African-American city kids, but in order to avoid an argument that would certainly inflame my headache, I slipped into my one nice outfit: a pair of maroon loafers, Dockers khakis, white shirt, and a tie.

We arrived at the four-way stop near the high school at a right angle and simultaneous to a classic, rodded-out, black 1967 Buick Sport station wagon in impossibly-mint condition. The low, long. and lean lines of the wagon gave it a hearse-like appearance. Somehow it was both lame and bad ass.

I had slouched so low in my seat – my default position whenever being chauffeured by my mom – that I was surprised when the driver of the Buick apparently recognized me and waved. I don't know how he could even have seen me to know I was there.

"That man is waving at you, honey," my mom stated the obvious.

"I can see that, Mom."

"Who is he?"

I rose in my seat and peered through the windshield and the dark. "It's Mr. Mortis. He's a substitute teacher. He's waving for you to go."

My mom visibly shuddered as she returned his wave.

"What was that?" I asked.

"I don't know. A shiver just ran up my spine, like someone stepped on my grave." She returned her attention to Mr. Mortis. "That man sure doesn't look like any teacher I've ever seen. He looks like that Scissorshands fella in that movie."

"That movie is older than I am."

"I'm just saying he's strange-looking, like one of those – what do you kids call 'em? – Goths?"

I rolled my eyes, sighed, and returned to my slouch. "Really, Mom? Goths?"

She entered the intersection and turned left in front of Mr. Mortis, who smiled and waved his scissors-less hand once again before accelerating into the fading black of the morning.

*****

It was still more dark than light when my mom dropped me off at the windowless, cement block locker room at 6:45. Coach Harris's and Coach McKuen's pickup trucks were already parked outside the steel front door. The pickup to car ratio in and around Goodness Falls was somewhere around four-to-one. I found them in the coaches' office already breaking down the previous night's game film. I knocked on the glass. Coach Harris waved me inside.

"We were just talking about you, Farrell," he said. "Look here." He directed the red dot from his laser pointer to the white board onto which the game film was being projected. "What in God's name were you thinking on this play right here before half? It's a simple choice route, son. We've got their backside defender isolated between two receivers. All you had to do was pick one."

Coach ran the play over and over and waited impatiently for my explanation. However, for the life of me, I could hardly remember the game much less a single play and my decision-making process. "I don't know, Coach. I guess I just screwed up."

Coach Harris exhaled a puff of disappointment. "Okay, Farrell." He paused the projector. "What can we do for you?"

"Dr. Stone is taking me on a recruiting visit to Toledo today. He thought I should take along a highlight disc to give to the coaches there."

"Is that right?" Coach Harris said, then he looked to Coach McKuen. "Coach, would you mind running up to the Get-Go for a couple of cups of coffee while I take care of Farrell here?"

Coach McKuen understood that, although it'd been politely framed as a question, he'd been given an order. He excused himself and quickly disappeared through the locker space and front door.

"The University of Toledo, huh?" Coach Harris asked as he rose from behind his desk. "I thought they'd already passed on you."

"I thought so too, but I guess Dr. Stone has some connections or something like that."

"Isn't that nice," Coach said without even a feeble attempt to hide his sarcasm. He walked to the wall and flipped on the overhead light, which caused me to squint as protection against the searing burn of the fluorescent bulb against my retinas.

"You okay, Farrell? You look a little pekid."

"I got my bell rung pretty good on that last play. I guess I'm still a little woozy."

"Why don't you sit down?"

I took Coach McKuen's vacated chair.

"Did you know that this is the thirtieth year I've coached high school football?"

"No, sir. I didn't."

"I've had plenty of opportunities to move on from Goodness Falls to bigger schools and even some offers to join college staffs, but I've always turned them down."

"I'm glad you did," I lied.

"Do you know why?"

"No, sir."

"I stayed because of my son, Donny. You remember Donny. Don't you, Farrell?"

"Yes, sir. I went to school with him for eleven years."

"That's right. You did. Donny always loved it here, and he loved Ducks football even more. Since the day he could walk, he spent every minute he could with me and around this football program. It was our dream that, one day, he'd be the Ducks quarterback and I'd coach him." He leaned back in his chair and locked his hands behind his head as if he were afraid that, otherwise, he might reach across the desk and strangle me. "We both know what happened to that dream. Don't we, Farrell?"

"Yes, sir." I said and left it at that.

"Do you know what Donny's doing now?"

I was tempted to say "mostly drugs and skanky sophomores," but I said, "No, sir. I don't."

"Absolutely nothing. Sleeps all morning. Plays video games most of the afternoon, and disappears out the back door the minute he sees my truck coming down the street. Do you have any idea how that makes a father feel?"

I didn't know what to say, but none of Coach's disappointment was my fault and I wasn't about to cop to it.

"Well, I've decided I'm ready to retire from teaching, get my family on out of Goodness Falls, and maybe take one of those college coaching jobs. And it just so happens, I have a few connections of my own on the football staff at Toledo. Some old markers to cash in you might call it. And it sure wouldn't hurt if maybe you'd say some good things to Coach Markinson and maybe even to Dr. Stone. I know he works at the medical college there and is a big alumni donor. The way I see it, the two of you owe me at least that much."

"Yes, sir. I can do that," I said; although, I didn't mean it. Four more years with Coach Harris would be unbearable.

"That's fine," he said. "Let me get you that disc."

The sound of a car horn blared from the parking lot.

"That's my ride," I said.

Coach Harris put a meaty hand on my shoulder and walked me to the door. He opened it just wide enough to let me out, stuck his head through the opening, and flashed a phony smile at Dr. Stone, where he sat inside his obsidian black metallic-colored Mercedes Benz CLS 550 Coupe. (No one knows more about cars than a licensed teenage boy who doesn't own one.) Coach raised his hand as a sort of wave, and Dr. Stone half-acknowledged it with a slight backwards nod of his head. Under his breath, I heard Coach Harris mutter, "Asshole."

*****

Dr. Stone released the power locks and pointed to the rear driver's side door. I thought it odd, but I climbed in back. An opened briefcase, iPad, and iPhone were positioned on the front passenger seat. "Good Morning," I said.

"Got the highlight disc?"

"Yes."

"Good." He took a long look at me in the rear view mirror. "You feeling alright? You don't look too good."

"A little tired that's all. I didn't sleep so good last night."

"They probably won't ask, but don't volunteer anything regarding your history with concussions. That'll red flag you faster than a fifteen on your A-C-T. You have taken it, haven't you?"

"Yes, sir. I got a twenty-one."

Dr. Stone harrumphed his disappointment in my less-than-mediocre score as if he were already imagining his daft grandchildren.

He turned the Benz around in the nearly empty lot and made towards the exit. The football complex sat a quarter of the way down a long, sloping hill on Business Route 101. At that early hour on a Saturday, not a person stirred nor a single light shone from any of the houses across the road. I suppose, being a doctor, Dr. Stone was often in a hurry and more-or-less expected the world to get out of his way. So I wasn't surprised when he made a sharp left turn onto BR 101 without coming to anything resembling a complete stop. I *was*, however, surprised by the blast of air horn, the scream of air brakes, and the sight of the massive front tires and the chrome grill of an eighteen-wheeled semi bearing down on me. At the moment before collision, my eyes telescoped onto the license plate: TJ 1027. It was literally the intended instrument of my death, an eighteen-wheeled bullet with my name and death date inscribed on it.

Dr. Stone accelerated the Benz through the turn onto the road and carried me safely past the hard-charging semi. As it roared past, on the driver side door of the truck, I read, "Mooseburger Trucking." It was Moose's dad. He had been a farmer for over twenty years, but after too many seasons of low crop yields and break-even prices, he sold the farm and turned to short and long haul trucking for his living. Before we were totally clear, the truck's fender grazed the rear passenger side panel of the Benz.

"Holy shit!" Dr. Stone yelled. "Asshole! No Thru Trucks! Can't you read the goddamned sign!"

Ignoring Dr. Stone's warped interpretation of the events leading to the near catastrophe, I turned and, in the hellish red glare of brake lights, saw that the semi, unlike us, was not yet out of danger. Mr. Mooseburger had swung wide to the right onto the soft shoulder and had made the mistake of overcorrecting. Nine of eighteen wheels were airborne and the trailer was careening at nearly forty-five degrees. I gasped and watched as Mr. Mooseburger managed to right the truck and land it back on its full complement of tires. However, as it neared the bottom of the hill, where the business route t-boned back into the State Route 101, the truck ran the stop sign and barreled straight into a massive oak tree in the front yard of the Thompson family, whose twin, seven-year old sons shared a bedroom that would have been obliterated had not that oak tree stopped the truck.

"Shouldn't we stop and see if he's alright?"

Dr. Stone ignored – if he even heard – me. "Bastard almost killed us. Goddamned truckers think they own the road," Dr. Stone said. I don't think he even thought to stop or to turn around and check on the truck, Mr.

Mooseburger, or the Thompson family. I'm not sure he ever even looked in his rear view mirror.

Other than Dr. Stone making and taking phone calls and texts and turning up some progressive jazz station on the satellite radio in the intervals between them, we drove the forty miles or so to campus in silence. I turned on my iPod, slipped in my ear buds, and tried to lose myself in the music, but by the time we arrived on campus, it was clear that something in Dr. Stone's arrogant demeanor had changed. He'd grown fidgety in his seat. His free hand made stress runs over the back of his neck and his morning stubble, and his eyes inspected me repeatedly in the rearview mirror. After he'd parked outside of the admissions building, together we inspected the side of the Benz where the truck's fender had swiped a wide swath of paint off of her. "Goddamn it!" Dr. Stone said, climbed abruptly back into her, and disappeared without a word of explanation.

An admissions counselor gave me and the other recruits a tour of the campus then handed us off to a representative from the bursar's office. She had a stack of forms for us to fill out and sign. She passed us on to a graduate assistant from the football team who took all of us to brunch in the team cafeteria and gave each of us a combination locker room/sideline pass.

Dr. Stone reappeared on the sidelines late in the third quarter. Oddly, he smelled of perfume. "Coach Markinson is coming to the playoff game on Friday. Play well and you're in," he said then left me on the sideline. He spent the rest of the game in a luxury box high above the fifty yard line. After the game, we drove home in a different car, a red Audi A5 Cabriolet. It was sporty but kind of a chick car. I thought it unusual, but I lacked the balls to ask what he'd done with the Benz. Besides, he was clearly in no mood for an interrogation. The Cabriolet was a two door, but Dr. Stone directed me to the backseat once again, and we returned as we'd come, together alone.

From the solitary confinement of my cramped space, I texted the good news to Caly and lied about what a good time I'd had with her father, going so far as to say, "He's a lot nicer than I'd thought." I didn't mention that he'd nearly killed me before we'd escaped Goodness Falls.

"I told you so," she texted then added, "You haven't heard. Have you?"

"Heard what?" I responded.

"It's horrible."

"?"

"There was an accident. Moose is dead. His dad is in a coma."

I didn't respond. It had never crossed my mind that Moose would have been with his dad. I deleted the text as if that would somehow make the news untrue. I turned off my phone, turned up my iPod, stared out the window, and hid my tears from what had become Dr. Stone's continually prying eyes in the rear view mirror. The throbbing in my temples accelerated with reinvigorated intensity.

Chapter Three

Saturday Evening, October 27, 201_

It was after seven p.m. when Dr. Stone and I drove past the football stadium on Lowell street and turned right at the four-way where it intersected with BR 101, the same spot where I had seen Mr. Mortis just over twelve hours earlier. Even in the dying light, the black skid marks on the road and the tire tracks on the shoulder were clear indicators of Mr. Mooseburger's evasive maneuvers. At the bottom of the hill in the Thompson's front yard, yellow police tape cordoned off the area around the oak tree, where the semi had come to rest. A garden of bouquets of flowers, balloons, and stuffed animals had bloomed around the trunk of the bowed oak. Someone had spelled "R.I.P. Moose #54" by sticking white Styrofoam cups into the holes in the chain link fence that surrounded the football complex. The orange-yellow security light over the door to the locker room was the only non-natural light shining in the lot. Beneath it, my dad sat inside his Ranger. The occasional orange-red glow from his cigarette betrayed his presence.

Dr. Stone pulled into the lot, smiled weakly, and waved to my dad, but instead of dropping me off, he stopped and shifted the Cabriolet into park. "What's your old man doing these days? Is he working?" He asked, staring in the pickup's direction.

"No," I said.

"I know some people. Maybe I could find him something."

I didn't respond.

Dr. Stone shifted his eyes so that he glared at me through the rear view mirror. "T.J.," he said in a foreboding tone, "we need to talk."

"I already know."

"I'm not talking about Moose. We need to get our story straight about the accident," he said.

"What about it?" I asked through the fast-calcifying hatred, which I'd been able to suppress in isolation but was exacerbated by the sound of his voice.

"Things are bad enough. I don't see what good will come by telling anyone what we witnessed this morning."

"What we *witnessed*? *We* didn't witness it. I witnessed it. You caused it." My hands instinctively rolled into fists.

"That's not how I remember it. The way I see it, the Mooseburger family has suffered enough. If we report his reckless driving and by some miracle Mr. Mooseburger recovers, he could lose his trucking license. How will the family survive then? And how will he live with the guilt? As it stands now, it was simply a horrible accident."

"But it wasn't his fault! It was yours. You didn't even look. You just pulled right out onto the road." An unfamiliar rage boiled inside of me. I did my best to contain it. "Mr. Mooseburger saved my life by swerving. He could have plowed right into us and walked away without a scratch. And that's exactly what he'll tell the police when he wakes up."

"*If* he wakes up, and *if* he even remembers the accident," Dr. Stone said.

"Then I'll tell."

"You were sleepy and not feeling well. The light was bad, and from the backseat, you couldn't see as well as you think you did."

"I know what I saw, and it's exactly what I'm going to tell Chief Johnson and anyone who asks."

"Is that right? That's funny, because it doesn't sync with what I remember." His patience with me had worn thin. "And which of us do you suppose Chief Johnson is going to believe when there were no other witnesses?"

He was right. I didn't know what to say.

"Then there's this. Let's say you are right, and the Chief believes you and charges me. If I were to be convicted of vehicular manslaughter, how many more people's lives will be ruined? I'd most likely go to jail and lose everything in a lawsuit. What would happen to Caly and her mother? To Caly's plans for college and med school? How would she feel about her boyfriend testifying in court against her daddy? And what about you? What good would it do you? You could kiss your scholarship goodbye. Think of how that would devastate your mother."

I didn't answer. What was there to say? He was right.

"Look, T.J." He softened his tone. "I'm as torn up about this as you are, and trust me, if my admitting to your version of events would somehow bring David Mooseburger back or pull his father out of his coma, I'd go to Chief Johnson myself. But neither of those things are going to happen. The best thing we can do – the best thing for everybody – is to say nothing."

"What about the car?"

"Excuse me?"

"What about the Mercedes? How are you going to explain the damage?"

"Damage? I don't know what you're talking about. She's been running a little funny lately if that's what you mean. I'd planned all along to leave her with a mechanic friend in Toledo. I thought I'd mentioned that. There's no one around here who knows foreign engines. This Cabriolet is a loaner."

To think that he'd almost had me convinced that his concern was for the Mooseburgers. But his blatant lies regarding the damaged rear panel of the Mercedes and the Cabriolet and the length to which he had already gone to cover his tracks made it clear that his only concern was saving his own ass. My head spun, and I suddenly felt nauseous and short of breath.

"When did you find out?" I asked.

"I got a text before we even reached campus. Mr. Mooseburger was taken to my hospital. I checked in on him after I dropped you off."

"And you didn't bother to tell me?"

"I figured you'd want to hear from someone other than me."

"I need to go. My dad's waiting." Trapped in the back seat, however, I was totally at his mercy.

Dr. Stone reached his hand back between the seats for me to shake. "Are we in agreement then?"

At that point, I'd have said or done just about anything to escape that car. I shook his hand, and he released the automatic door locks.

I hurried to my dad's truck. The passenger side door cried out for oil when I swung it open. I climbed in and settled into the deep, ass-shaped compression in the bench seat. The vinyl cover was torn so that what was left of the foam cushion beneath oozed through to the surface. The air inside the cab of the pickup reeked of years' worth of cigarette smoke and self-pity. My feet fought for space with a Styrofoam cooler, spent beer cans, dip tins, and empty plastic bottles of motor oil.

"What was all that about?" My dad asked as he started the reluctant engine.

"Moose is dead, Dad. Moose is dead." I covered my face and sobbed uncontrollably into my hands.

My dad reached over and patted my knee. "There's beer in the cooler if you want one."

Although my family lived in the Goodness Falls school district, we did not live in the village. Rather, I grew up just inside the border of Crystal Ridge, a township along a short bend of the southern shore of the Sandusky Bay in Lake Erie's western basin. Originally, most of Crystal Ridge's residents were Daltons, the crossed lines of no more than six or seven families who'd come North from the Appalachian coal fields long ago. However, having all but drained their homegrown pool, recent generations had taken to intermarrying with migrant Mexican illegals desperate for permanent citizenship. Thinking they were clever, many in Goodness Falls referred to the hybrid products of the unlikely interbreeding as "Red backs" or "Wet necks" –   never to their faces.

The Dalton clan mostly made their meager livings by trolling for near shore minnows, which they sold to bait stores. A few of the Chicano lines still hired themselves out to area farmers. In the wintertime, with the lake frozen and the fields fallow, the entire family went on unemployment unapologetically. Pocked with homes amounting to little more than fishing shacks, Crystal Ridge possessed the aura of a third world shanty town. We weren't Daltons and my dad hated the water, but the non-waterfront homes in Crystal Ridge, like ours, and the property taxes they demanded were among the most affordable in Erie County. Our tiny house sat at the intersection of state route six and Hill Rd., which was one of only two ingresses into Crystal Ridge.

My mom met me at the back door when my dad and I arrived home. She tried to hug me, but I was in even less of a mood for her pity than for my dad's lack of it. I shrugged her off and headed straight for my bedroom in the low-ceilinged converted attic of our one story dump. "I have a headache," I offered by way of honest explanation. "C'mon, boy," I called to Bo, our border collie, whom I passed lying in his fleece, wraparound dog bed in the tiny living room. He immediately jumped to his feet, followed me up the stairs, climbed onto my twin bed, and settled in at the foot after performing a few proprietary turns.

I swear, for the next few hours, my phone vibrated nearly every fifteen seconds, but I had no desire for conversation or condolences. I let it buzz and ignored each call or text.

Around midnight, my mom appeared in my bedroom doorway. She stood silhouetted against the nightlight at the top of the narrow stairs. Atypically hesitant to barge into my room, she cupped something in her hands folded at her chest.

"What do you want, Mom?" I rolled onto my side away from her and the excruciating burn of the nightlight at the top of the stairs.

"You're flopping around up here like a fish on the dock. Does your head still hurt?"

"A little. I'm fine. It'll go away. It always does."

"You don't think you had another concussion, do you? Did Schultzie say anything? Does it feel like the last time?"

"I just got my bell rung, Mom. Don't worry about it. The last time was over a month ago."

"And the time before that?"

"I don't remember."

"I have these," she said hesitantly then revealed the amber pill bottle she'd been concealing in her hands. "They're left over from my root canal. They'll help you sleep."

"Sure. Whatever."

I sat up in bed and she handed me one of the white pills. I washed it down with the warm remains of a bottle of Gatorade. I wished there was a pill to take away the pain of Moose's death, but that hurt was heart deep and permanent. Maybe it was because I had never before taken a pill stronger than an over-the-counter aspirin, but the effects were incredible. Within a half hour, the pain in my head disappeared, a warm euphoria flowed through my veins, and I welcomed the sweet onset of sleep.

The din of machinery inside the windowless Erie Dressed Beef meat processing plant is constant and deafening. No matter what the preachers and poets say, Hell is brightly-lit, white, and cold. Its walls, exposed rafters, ceiling, and floor are all blanched white. Satan's minions hide their tails beneath white, knee-length coats and their horns under white-mesh hairnets and white hard hats. Handheld meat hooks, used to help move pinkish half-carcasses along the miles of overhead rails that snake through the plant, emanate from one or the other of their coat sleeves.

I am one of them. "Thomas" is stitched in blood red thread on the left breast of my butcher's coat. "This is a mistake," I say as I approach the worker next to me on the line and tap him on the shoulder with the curved side of my hook. "I don't work here. This is my dad's coat. This is my dad's life. Besides, this placed closed years ago."

Bizarrely, it's Mr. Mortis, the substitute English teacher, who turns to face me. "This place never closes," he smiles and says.

"Mr. Mortis!? What are you doing here?"

"Which 'here' do you mean, T.J.? In Goodness Falls? Or inside your head?"

"I don't understand."

"You will," he says cryptically.

I turn and watch several sides of beef, suspended from meat hooks on the overhead rails, swing past. "It's strange," I say, "to think that yesterday these cows were grazing in some farmers' fields. Some of them could even be Brian Tucker's. You know Brian, Mr. Mortis. He's a year behind me at school. His family raises cattle."

"I know the grandmother," Mr. Mortis says. "I've yet to meet the rest of the family."

Over Mr. Mortis's shoulder, something odd coming down the rails grabs my attention. "What's that?" I ask.

He turns toward where I point. "Looks like I'm up," he says instead of answering.

Naked, grey-blue, and hanging from meat hooks that pierce their trapezius muscles, two human corpses come swinging down the rails separated by one empty hook and followed by two others. I recognize the first as Mr. Miller's wife, who had died unexpectedly of a brain aneurysm and precipitated Mr. Mortis' serving as our long term sub. The second is Moose. Their eyes are wide open and their pink gums are exposed through their dropped jaws.

Mr. Mortis raises his meat hook and . . .

Chapter Four

Sunday Morning, October 28, 201_

I woke in a shivering start, flat on my back, and attempting to sort nightmare from fact. I stared at the galaxy of burnt out, glow-in-the-dark, plastic stars my mom and I had pressed against the ceiling when I was eight years old. In the familiarity of that space and throughout the climb to full-consciousness, except for a low grade thumping in my head, I concluded that all was still right with my world. I hadn't become my father – at least, not yet. My future was still undetermined and ahead of me. Then I remembered Moose. His wasn't. I broke out into a cold sweat and struggled to breathe. I threw my blankets to the floor, gasped for air, and puked in my cylindrical, aluminum Cleveland Browns trash can.

When the panic attack had passed, my throat was on fire, my eyes burned, and the throbbing had resumed full-on inside my head. I removed a pair of boxers, jeans, and my favorite hoodie from a wash basket. The black hoodie's string had been lost long ago, the cuffs were frayed, and I'd purposefully torn a short seam at the throat when my shoulders and chest broadened two summers earlier. With Bo at my heels, I plugged my nose, grabbed the trash can, and headed downstairs, where I tiptoed past my father in his default position: passed out and snoring on the couch.

While Bo relieved himself in the side yard, I set the can outside the back door and filled his food and water bowls in the tiny rear mud room. I brushed my teeth and washed up in the downstairs bathroom while Bo finished his breakfast. Returning the toothpaste to the shelf inside the mirror-faced medicine cabinet, I noticed my mom's nearly-full, amber-colored pill bottle. I stole two of the magic tablets. One I took immediately; the other I stashed in my pocket and saved for later.

The keys to the pickup lay on the kitchen counter; I snatched them and slid into my high-top tennis shoes and a red, faded nearly to pink, Farmall Tractors ball cap. Once out of the backdoor, I crossed the scraggly, browning grass to where the truck was parked in front of our dilapidated barn at the end of the gravel-strewn driveway. There was nothing I could do to muffle the grumpy complaint of the truck. All I could hope was that my father was too drunk to be roused by the engine and my mother too fat and slow to reach me before I pulled away.

Caly and I had been together since spring of our sophomore year, exactly one year, five months and twenty-eight days. I had no conscious memory of asking her out for a first date or asking her to be my steady girlfriend. We'd just sort of spun in the same circles until our lines of orbit blurred, nature ran its course, and we melded into a couple.

The Stones lived in Willow Brook Estates, a bedroom community without a single willow tree or a brook. Carved out of what was farmland no more than fifteen years earlier, the subdivision sat to the west of the village limits in an annexed township. The homes in Willow Brook all wore some variation of a brick front and sat back off the street, far removed from even the nearest neighbors. A three-car garage minimum seemed to be strictly enforced, and every house had a manicured lawn and professionally designed and maintained landscaping.

When I turned into the subdivision, the cranky, old pickup sputtered as if it were aware of our conspicuous and unwelcome intrusion. Several early morning dog walkers carrying plastic bags of shit actually had the nerve to turn up their noses at me. I mean, I may have been some kind of hick in their eyes, but at least I didn't wipe my dog's ass.

Up the street, I saw that someone had already backed the Escalade out of the Stone's garage. It waited to chariot them to their regular 9:00 a.m. Sunday mass at St. Mary's Catholic Church in nearby Sandusky. The back end of the Cabriolet was visible through the still-open garage door. It looked as inappropriately placed in the family-friendly environs of Willow Brook as a pair of ruby red, high-heeled stilettos on an Amish girl's closet floor.

The Stones emerged from behind their oaken front door just as I arrived. I pressed the brake and came to a stop at the foot of their driveway. Performing a nearly-perfectly synchronized halt, the Stones trio momentarily studied each other's inclinations and waited for one of the others to make the next move.

Caly broke for the truck.

I hated myself for noticing, but in her brown riding boots, matching tights, and curve-hugging, long-sleeved, ivory, cable knit sweater-dress, she was drop dead gorgeous.

"Caly!" Her mother called. "Get back here! It's Sunday."

"Let her go," Mr. Stone said and ended her protest. He proceeded around to the driver's side of the Escalade, leaving his wife to open her own door and to climb unassisted into the massive SUV.

Without a word of hello or explanation, I performed a u-turn in the middle of the street and escaped from Willow Brook.

Caly let out a cathartic scream. "Why didn't you answer my calls or texts? I was so worried about you! My father hid the keys to all of our cars to keep me from driving out to your house."

"I couldn't talk. I needed some time to think," I said.

"Don't you ever shut me out like that again," Caly warned from behind a wagging finger then settled into her seat. She tried to play it off, but she was clearly concerned with what may rub off of the Ranger's grimy interior onto her outfit. She tugged on the hem of her sweater-dress before pulling the shoulder strap across her front in a way that it bisected her breasts. "Where are we going?"

"Your dad's hospital. You know the way right?" I asked and returned my attention to the road.

"Of course. I've been there a million times. But why?"

"I have to see Mr. Mooseburger."

"Moose's dad? Why?"

"I don't know. I just need to. And I need to tell Moose's mom I'm sorry."

"Do you think this," she hesitated, parsed her choice of nouns and settled for the most generous, "truck will make it?"

"I'm not sure. I guess we're going to find out. Your father said Mr. Mooseburger is in a coma."

"They life-flighted him from the accident scene," she explained.

"We were supposed to go duck hunting yesterday."

"You and Mr. Mooseburger?"

"No. Moose and me. We'd been planning it all year. We'd agreed that on the Saturday after the last regular season game and before the weather turned and the playoffs started, we were going to go duck hunting in Resthaven. But I went to Toledo with your father instead. That's why Moose was helping his dad. If I wouldn't have cancelled our hunting trip, he wouldn't have been in that truck, and he'd still be alive."

"Teege. You can't think like that. You can't blame yourself."

I thought, *If only she knew who I could blame*, but I kept it to myself. "So what happened?" Although I obviously knew the truth, I fished for details on whatever story was making the rounds regarding the accident.

"From what I've heard, Mr. Mooseburger must have lost control of the truck outside the football stadium. Maybe it was some kind of a mechanical problem.

Maybe he had a heart attack or something. I don't think they know yet. But he ran the stop sign and crashed into a tree in the Thompson's front yard."

"Then what?"

"I don't know. Someone must have called 9-1-1. Probably the Thompsons."

"What about Moose?"

"I don't really know."

"That old semi didn't even have seatbelts. They both must have hit their heads pretty hard," I said, then surprised Caly and myself with an inappropriate laugh.

She smiled nervously. "Why are you laughing?"

"Moose. He had the hardest head ever. Before big games, to get everyone fired up, he would take his helmet off and head butt guys still wearing theirs. Sometimes blood would be running down his forehead, but he'd just smile this crazy smile and laugh like some kind of psycho. He was crazy." I laughed again at the memory, but the laughter soon turned to tears. I was forced to wipe my cheeks and nose with the sleeve of my hoodie. "I miss him so much already. He had my back, you know? I always knew he had my back."

Caly undid the shoulder belt, slid across the seat, put her arms around my neck, and kissed the side of my face. "It's okay, baby. It'll all be okay. I have your back. I'll always have your back. Thanks to Daddy, we're going to go to school together. After graduation, you'll get a job while I finish med school, then we're going to get married, live in a big house, and have lots of babies."

I squirmed at her mention of "Daddy," and coldly suggested, "You should put your seat belt back on."

Each semi that passed us on the turnpike rattled the old pickup and us inside. Each was a cold reminder of Moose, his father, and the fragility of our own lives.

"What about arrangements?" I asked.

"I don't know for sure. Talk is that the showing will be on Tuesday and the funeral on Wednesday. There's going to be a students-only vigil at the stadium tonight, and a bunch of seniors are getting together at Brian Tucker's afterward. What about the game?" Caly changed the subject. "Do you think we'll play?"

I shot her a look of shocked disbelief. Caly correctly read my dismay at her skewed priorities.

"I'm just asking. You know this town. There's nothing more important than Ducks football. Plus, this is the start of the state playoffs."

"You're right," I conceded. "I can hear Coach Harris' bullshit already: 'Moose would have wanted us to play. Let's win one for Moose!'"

"Would he have wanted us to play?"

"I don't know what he would have wanted. A lot of the way he acted was just David being Moose. Moose probably would say, 'Hell yeah! Go on and play, boys. Kick some ass! But David? I'm not so sure. He was actually very sensitive, you know?"

"No, I don't. I never knew that side of Moose. I wish I had."

"It's like when we'd fish, he'd only use lures, never live worms, and I never once saw him keep anything he caught. He'd remove the hook as gently as he could and set the fish just as gently back into the water. And when we'd go hunting, he had to be either the worst shot in the world or he purposefully shot over the ducks, because I don't remember him once getting one. I guess, he just liked being outdoors and with me," my voice trailed off as I hid my tears by feigning interest in my side view mirror. "And now he's dead."

"I know. It doesn't seem fair."

"Coach Harris says, 'Fare is what you pay the bus driver. In life, there is no fair.' I guess he's right."

"Here's our exit," Caly said, ignoring my resignation to Coach Harris's pitiless worldview.

We had to scrounge around in the ash tray, on the floor, and between and under the seat in order to come up with the $1.35 toll. The booth attendant stuck out her palm and received the grimy and lint-smeared coins with something less than enthusiasm.

*****

The University of Toledo Medical Center is a teaching hospital with the finest level one trauma center in Northwest Ohio and Southeastern Michigan. Caly decided to wait in the truck while I went inside. "I'm no good at this sort of thing," she said.

I told her she was already halfway-qualified to being a doctor then. She didn't think it funny.

"I won't be long. I just need to see Moose's mom. Tell her I'm sorry," I said.

"Remember what I told you. I have your back now."

"From the truck?"

"You know what I mean," Caly said.

"Fifteen minutes. I promise."

As I entered the main lobby, I ran directly into Ken Johnson, the chief of the four-man Village of Goodness Falls police force, exiting. There was no way of avoiding him. Besides, to do so may have sparked his curiosity.

"Hey, Chief," I said, doing my best to avoid looking into his eyes or to give him a long look into mine.

"T.J." He reached out his hand to shake. "It's good of you to come all this way, but good luck getting past the charge nurse. 'Immediate family only,' she says. She wouldn't let me anywhere near Wayne. That's, uh, Mr. Mooseburger."

"I know. How's he doing?" I asked while studying my shoe tops.

"Well, I spoke to the Mrs., but she's still pretty much in shock herself. Really couldn't get much out of her other than Wayne took a nasty blow to the head. She called it a traumatic brain injury. The brain's swollen pretty bad and causing all sorts of pressure on the brain stem. He's in a coma."

"When he comes out of it, will he be able to remember the accident?" I asked.

"Funny you ask that. I had the same question for the nurse. She said no two cases are the same. When and if he comes to, he most likely won't remember a single thing about it. Over time, it may come back to him in bits and pieces, but son, it's only the machines keeping him alive."

"That sucks," I said taking sudden ocular interest in the butt of the service revolver inside the holster strapped to his hip.

"Yes, it does. It's a tragedy really. I can't imagine what caused Wayne to lose control of that rig. He'd been driving trucks bigger than that since he was a boy."

"Maybe," I said, "something spooked him. It is bow season. There are a lot of deer moving around at dawn."

"Could be, but old Wayne's never been the type to swerve for a deer. He'd be more likely to run it over, strap it to the hood, take it home, and gut it. Fill his freezer for winter."

"No witnesses?" I asked and made glancing eye contact before glaring into the sunshine streaming through the atrium ceiling.

"Nope. None that have come forward anyway. But come to think of it, Saturday morning, I was coming out of the Get-Go with a cup of coffee when Coach McKuen was coming in. He said that he'd just left you and Coach Harris at the locker room."

"I had to pick up a highlight disc. Caly's father took me on a recruiting visit to Toledo."

"Is that right? So are you going to be a Rocket?"

"I don't know. Maybe. Coach Markinson is coming to the game this Friday."

"You know? That would have been right around the time the 9-1-1 call came in."

"What? I mean, yes. I suppose. I don't know."

"They could use a dual-threat quarterback like you, if you ask me."

My head spun once more. "That's what they told me on my visit."

"I need to stop by and talk to Coach Harris, but I doubt that he could have heard or seen a thing inside that old bomb shelter of a locker room. I don't suppose, as you were leaving, with Dr. Stone you say?"

"Yes."

He took out a small notebook. I saw him write Dr. Stone's name inside.

"Caly Stone is my girlfriend. Her father is on staff here," I explained. "He knows a lot of influential people."

"Is that right? So, T.J., you and the doctor didn't happen to see the Mooseburgers' semi or anything or anyone else as you were walking to the car maybe or pulling out of the parking lot or even up the road? Anyone who may have seen the accident?"

I thought of seeing Mr. Mortis, but at that point, I had yet to make any connection. Beads of sweat formed on my forehead even in the cool atrium/lobby. I was uncomfortable with the Chief's line of questioning, and I didn't like the suspicion in his eyes. I felt the color flush from my face. It took every ounce of concentration to finally look him in the eyes and answer. "No, sir. I didn't see anything. We must have just missed them."

The Chief didn't immediately respond. Instead, he held my gaze for what seemed an eternity. "Well, okay then. It's fortuitous that I've run into you here. Now I won't need to bother you or your folks at home."

"Yes, sir."

"How'd you like that word by the way? Fortuitous."

"Huh?" I asked.

"Fortuitous. I have a word-of-the-day calendar on the dash of the cruiser. I learn one word a day and try to use it as much as I can as I go about my business. No better way to improve your vocabulary or to impress those you meet. You ought to get yourself one. You can put it on your desk in your dorm room at Toledo next year. Today's word is fortuitous."

"Maybe I'll do that, Chief."

"Alright. If you go on up, don't stay too long. Pay your respects and move on. Wayne's wife has a long week ahead of her. She's going to need all the strength she can muster."

The Chief wasn't kidding about the Nazi charge nurse. When the third floor elevator door opened, a large African-American woman in navy blue scrubs, sparkling white tennis shoes, and with an ID badge on a lanyard around her neck was waiting for me with arms crossed and feet and jaw set. Her badge read Chandra Owens, R.N.

"Who you here for?" She asked.

"Wayne Mooseburger."

"You family?"

"No, M'am." I said.

"Visitation is for family only in the ICU unit. Those are the rules."

"I'm friends with Mr. Mooseburger's son, David." My mention of his name hit me surprisingly hard. Once again, my eyes began to tear and my nose to run.

My display of emotion must have softened her resolve. "Wait right here," Nurse Owen said. She then punched a large silver disc on the wall that opened the glass maw of the ICU unit, and she disappeared inside. A few minutes later, she reappeared behind the glass and reentered the elevator lobby. "Your auntie says you can come on back."

"Oh, no," I corrected her. "I said that I was . . ."

"*I* said your auntie says you can come on back."

I began once more to refute her mistaken notion, but Nurse Owens' plan suddenly dawned on me and I understood.

"Yes, M'am. My aunt. Thank you."

"Mrs. Mooseburger is in the visitor's lounge."

I followed Nurse Owens into the ICU unit. As we passed a darkened room, I saw a patient I believed to be Moose's dad, who weighed nearly three hundred pounds. He enveloped his mattress and seemed only to be held aloft by the tubes that tethered him to the various machines that hissed and beeped all around him. His head was heavily bandaged and his eyes swollen nearly shut, but there were no other signs of external injury – at least not I could see from where I stood in the hallway.

Mrs. Mooseburger sat on the edge of a wooden rocking chair with her feet flat on the floor in the darkened corner of the room. She stared out the window as if she'd already forgotten that Nurse Owens had told her that I was coming in to see her. She looked older and greyer than the last time I'd seen her just two days earlier serving desserts with the rest of the football moms at the pre-game team feed at the VFW. Her shoulders were slumped and the corners of her eyes and mouth were turned downward by the gravity of grief. Everything about her seemed to be being pulled towards the earth, where she would soon bury her son and, if Dr. Stone and Chief Johnson were correct, not long after, her husband would follow. Strangely, I felt the suction of her sinking myself. I wondered if the word crestfallen had ever shown up on the Chief's calendar.

"Hello, T.J.," Mrs. Mooseburger reanimated as if her grieving were somehow impolite or inappropriate for me to witness.

"Hi, Mrs. Mooseburger," I said.

She rose from her chair and immediately moved to comfort me, hugging me close and promising that it'd be okay.

"I'm so sorry," I said and cried onto her shoulder.

"There's nothing for you to be sorry for or anyone to be angry about. It was an accident."

The word 'accident' was like a kick to the balls of my conscience.

She held onto my hands but backed away. "I want to thank you for coming all the way up here. It means the world to me, and I'm sure David appreciates it as well." She clearly didn't have the desire or stamina for visitors.

"Will you be at the vigil tonight?" I asked.

No, honey. I'll be here with my husband. I need to be here when he wakes up."

"But the doctors . . ."

"I know what the doctors say, but what do they know about my husband? I say he's going to wake up. And mine will be the first face he sees when he does, and I will be the one to tell him his boy has gone home to the lord. My sister's come up from Zanesville way to tend to David's arrangements. Mr. Zucker from the funeral home has been wonderful. Now you be careful driving home and tell anyone who asks that I'm fine. And, T.J., me and the husband plan to follow you boys all the way to state, you hear?"

"Yes, M'am."

She hugged me one more time then shooed me on out the door.

Nurse Owens stopped me outside the elevators and insisted, "Don't you tell nobody about this."

I promised complete secrecy and made my way out of the hospital, stopping at a drinking fountain to take the second of the pills I'd stolen from my mother.

*****

After we were back on the road, traveling state routes and avoiding the turnpike without a penny to our names, Caly glanced over at me with a curious expression. "Why'd you say you wanted to tell Moose's mom that you were sorry? You said it twice."

"I don't know. It's just an expression."

"'I'm sorry for your loss' is the expression. You said, you were going to tell her *you* were sorry, like you were guilty of something."

"I don't know. I guess I didn't know what else to say."

Caly didn't appear satisfied by my answer, but she gave me the benefit of the doubt and soon fell asleep while I drove the remainder of the way back to Goodness Falls in pensive silence.

"Would you like to come in?" Caly asked when we arrived at her house.

"No. I better get the truck home."

"Pick you up for the vigil?"

"If you don't mind."

"Of course I don't mind," she said, slid over, and kissed me before climbing out of the Ranger and marching into her house.

*****

My mother met me at the back door holding my hosed-out Cleveland Browns paper can. "Where've you been? And what's with the puke? Are you sick, T.J.? I've been worried to death." She tried to sound stern and disapproving, but in our lives together, she'd never been able to stay angry with me. Her tone changed immediately to concern, and she hugged me like I was the Prodigal Son.

"I had to get out," I answered.

"You didn't answer your phone. I don't know why we pay for you to have a phone if you're not going to answer it."

I paid for my own phone with money I earned baling hay for the families of buddies on the team, but I didn't remind her. "I'm sorry. I must have left it on silent."

"Are you hungry? Sit down. Let me make you something."

My mother's idea of "making something" meant microwaving something or dumping something from a can into a pan and stirring that something around until it was hot. "No thanks. I'll just have a few cookies and maybe a glass of milk. I've got a headache. Could I have another one of those pills?"

She paused and considered my request then disappeared into the downstairs bathroom before returning with another tiny tablet.

"What are these anyway?" I asked.

"Vicodin," she whispered as if it were a dirty word and handed me the tablet. From off the counter, she took the Winnie-the-Pooh cookie jar full of store-bought cookies and placed it on the square card table that served as our kitchen table. She then poured me a tall glass of milk with which I greedily washed down the pill.

"Your dad got the best news while you were gone," she said, unable to contain her giddiness any longer.

"Yeah? What's that? They've made sitting on the couch watching redneck reality television an Olympic sport?"

"Don't talk like that about your dad."

"I'm sorry. I'm just upset."

"I know you are, honey," she said, but the affected sadness in her voice was being overwhelmed by her joy over whatever the good news was that my dad had received. She circled around the table, wrapped her thick, pink forearms around my chest and shoulders, pressed her watermelon breasts against the back of my neck, and pulled me into the vast chasm of her cleavage.

"Where is he anyway?" I asked while extricating my head from the canyon between her massive boobs.

"Because you ran off with the truck, he had to borrow Mr. Lewis's next door to go get a haircut." She uncoiled her boa constrictor arms, settled her pudgy fingers on my shoulders, and began to knead the muscles in my neck with her thumbs.

"Was he mad?"

"When have you ever seen your father angry?"

"Never. But I wish he'd get a little pissed off about something sometime."

"T.J. Farrell! Watch your mouth!" She said and released me entirely. She settled heavily into the chair next to mine. "I don't know where you pick up such gutter language. I hope you don't talk like that in public. Why, people will think we're trash like those bait-fishing, pot-smoking Daltons up the road."

"Pissed off? You think 'pissed off ' is 'gutter language,' and you think the Daltons are trash but we're not?"

"We are not trash. Your father has been laid off of work. He had a good job."

"*Had*, Mom. *Had* a good job. He's not 'laid off.' And the slaughterhouse is closed for good. There's no job to go back to."

"Times have been tough. It ain't like Opportunity's been knocking on the door and your dad's been refusing to answer. But," she said, and the optimistic lilt in her voice returned, "that's all about to change."

"How's that?"

"While you were out, Dr. Stone stopped by."

I bolted upright as if a jolt of electricity had coursed through my chair. "Here? He came here!?" It wasn't as if I didn't know that Caly's parents were aware of where I lived, but it was a whole another thing to have one of them actually inside my shithole of a house.

"Yes, he did, and he couldn't have been any nicer. In fact, that's why your dad had to go for a haircut. Dr. Stone wants him to come see him at the hospital in Toledo tomorrow. He's going to introduce your dad to the head of the maintenance department. He's pretty sure he can find him a job. Isn't that great? It ain't no minimum wage job neither, and he won't come home stinking of pig blood. We'll have real health insurance and everything. Can you believe it? I can finally get the rest of my teeth fixed."

I stared at Winnie, too stunned by the news and, I have to admit, too impressed by Dr. Stone's evil genius to speak.

"I said, isn't that great, T.J.!? Your daddy is finally going to be working again, and maybe, we can move out of Crystal Ridge and into the village or, maybe even, if you get that scholarship, we'll move up to Toledo to be closer to dad's work and to you. We'll be able to see all of your football games. Maybe, we'll even get you your own truck."

I continued to stare at the pot-bellied Winnie, hugging a honey jar close to his chest.

"What's the matter, sweetheart? I thought you'd be happy for your dad – for all of us."

"I am, Mom. I am. It's just . . . it's just that the scholarship isn't guaranteed. Coach Markinson is coming to the game on Friday. He may not think I'm good enough."

"Not good enough?" She repeated then stepped in close and pulled up the shoulders of my hoodie and brushed imaginary lint off of my chest. "One look at you on that football field and that coach will be begging you to go play for him. This is our time, T.J. I can feel it. I've been praying on it. The Farrells are back. This is our time," she repeated, "and it's all thanks to you and Dr. Stone. Now go get cleaned up. You snuck out of here this morning without showering or shaving. You look and smell like a good-for-nothing Dalton field hand. Get," she said and slapped me on the ass toward the bathroom.

"Okay," I agreed. "Caly's picking me up later. Some kids are getting together at the stadium for some kind of vigil for Moose then going to Brian Tucker's for a bonfire afterwards."

Chapter Five

Sunday, October 28, 201_

I watched for Caly through the front door window and rushed out to greet her before she could even think about stepping one foot out of the Escalade. What had been a pleasantly warm day for the end of October in Ohio had turned into a cool evening. I wore my varsity letter jacket over my typical plaid flannel, a pair of jeans, and untied work boots. The letter jacket had been a Christmas gift from Caly the previous year. She was dressed for mourning in all blacks and grays: black leather riding boots over black yoga pants with a black blouse covered by a long, sweeping, gray cardigan with a sash around her waist. Only her golden blond hair refused to join in the show of grief.

"So," I said after a kiss hello. "Your father is getting my dad a job."

"I haven't heard that. I haven't seen either of my parents. They're at some kind of fundraising dinner for the hospital. But I hope you're not offended," Caly said, backing out of the driveway.

"Offended? Why would I be offended?" I said sarcastically. "The Farrells are more than happy to become your father's favorite charity. First, he pulls some strings to get me a chance at a scholarship, then he does the impossible: he gets my father's lazy ass off the couch by finding him a job at the hospital where he works. My mom is inside building a shrine to the good Dr. Stone right now."

"Don't look at it like that."

"How else am I supposed to look at it?" I could feel myself growing uncharacteristically angry. I'd always been even-tempered, but I couldn't stop the anger from growing or stop myself from misdirecting it at Caly. None of it was her fault. I knew that. But she was there.

"See it as what friends do for one another," she said without a sniff of irony.

"Really? Friends? Should I be expecting my folks to be accompanying your parents to the next performance of the Toledo Symphonic at the Stranahan Theater, or will the Stones of Willow Brook be joining the Farrells of Crystal Ridge at the Monster Truck races at the Toledo Sports Arena? Isn't that something 'friends' do? Go on double dates."

Caly sighed. "Don't complicate it, T.J. Just let it be what it is: a good thing for everyone, especially for us. So my father wants to do something nice for yours; can't you leave it at that?"

"I wish that's all it was," I said in a muffled voice that Caly still managed to hear.

"What's that supposed to mean?" With two hands draped over the top of the steering wheel, her attention bounced back and forth from me to the road. "What could my father possibly have to gain by doing your father a favor?"

"Gee, thanks."

"I didn't mean it like that. You're being too sensitive and over-thinking this. The way I see it, my father's coming to accept that you and I love each other and plan to be together for the rest of our lives. He's doing all he can to make that possible. Why can't you just be grateful?"

"I guess I'm just not used to his generosity. He spent the first year trying to break us up. Remember?"

Caly softened her tone. "That's what all daddies do when their little girls start bringing boys around, especially those with whom their daughters fall in love." She reached over, squeezed my hand, then turned east onto State Route 6 and headed toward the stadium.

The football stadium lay nestled in a natural, horseshoe-shaped hollow across the street from the high school. Both the visitors' and the home side bleachers were etched into the sides of sharply angled slopes. The south end of the stadium was a grassy hillside on top of which sat the football locker room and its parking lot. The north end was open to form an amphitheater. A six-foot high, chain link fence encircled the entire stadium property. By the time we arrived, a large crowd of students had already gathered in the parking lot.

It turned out that the evening's students-only vigil hadn't been as spontaneously-generated as I'd been led to believe. The not-so-impromptu gathering had actually been the joint brainchild of the three protestant churches in Goodness Falls. Youth ministers and the pastors from each worked the gathering. Some poured cups of hot chocolate. Others moved through the crowd and offered hugs and condolences. They all handed out white votive candles and circulated flyers inviting currently un-churched kids to their weekly youth services. Dressed in generic tennis shoes and button-down shirts, which they tucked snugly into their high-waisted blue jeans, they all tried hard, too hard, to look cool, but they looked plain ridiculous.

For an hour or so, not much happened except kids milled around and gathered in small groups for hugs and commiseration. I think a majority of the boys were just taking advantage of the situation and copping feels. By seven o'clock, my headache was back with a vengeance, and all of the candles were lit in anticipation of mourners completing a slow and silent lap on the track around the field in tribute to Moose.

Someone had gotten a hold of his white road jersey. I watched it being passed through the crowd. I just knew it would somehow end up in my possession, and I'd be expected to lead the procession, but I didn't want it. As quarterback with Moose as my center ever since we started playing Pee-Wee football together, my hands had spent more hours pressed against his crotch than I cared to think about, but I wanted nothing to do with touching his jersey now that he was dead, and I didn't want to lead anything or anyone. I wasn't a leader. I was a liar and a coward. But, sure-as-shit the jersey arrived, and there I was holding the #54 jersey at arm's length as if Moose's death were contagious and its germs were smeared all over it.

"I can't," I whispered to Caly. A brilliant, white light suddenly flashed behind my eyeballs and a giant black squid of a migraine rose from the depths, wrapped its tentacles around my skull, and squeezed.

"You're the team captain, and you were his best friend. You have to," she insisted.

"I can't," I said once more and let the jersey slip through my fingers to the ground. All who had been watching, voyeuristically expecting a tender moment, gasped. "I can't breathe," I said, and seeing a welcoming light seeping out from beneath the door of the locker room, I sought its sanctuary.

Once inside, I sat for a long time in the senior section of lockers in front of my cubicle next to Moose's catching my breath and taking an inventory of all that he left behind: playbook, a scouting report for Greene County, knee wraps, padded lineman's gloves, cleats, knee and thigh pads, shoulder pads, a helmet, deodorant, soap, a spirit bag half-filled with candy, several empty Gatorade bottles, a few letters from D-III football programs, and a mix-CD of Eminem songs. It was our pump-up music. We'd each burned the songs to our individual iPods long ago, but right before we left the locker room before games, we'd each take one ear bud connected to the same iPod and crank up "Lose Yourself."

I removed the CD from his locker and inserted it into the communal boom box that had been sitting on one of the training tables ever since Friday night. I inserted the disc and forwarded to "Lose Yourself." Eminem testified, "You better lose yourself in the music, the moment / You own it, you better never let it go." In what was becoming an embarrassing habit, tears formed in the corners of my eyes.

"I hate that song," Coach Harris's voice shocked and cut through me. "I only let you guys listen to that crap because it seems to fire you up."

I pressed "Stop" and tried to hide my face and tears. Coach Harris was the last person in the world I needed to see me cry. "Sorry, Coach. I didn't know you were here. I . . . um . . . I needed to get something from my locker."

"Is that right," he said and looked over toward the senior lockers. "Losing Mooseburger was the last thing I needed at the start of the playoffs."

"That's a little cold," I said.

"Cold is it? Let me tell you something, Farrell. Halfway through last season — you might remember this — on a Sunday evening just like this one, I was called to this locker room for a meeting, more like an ambush really. Dr. Stone and the boosters, Wayne Mooseburger was one of them as a matter of fact, wanted to talk to me about my coaching. They said I was making my decisions based on emotions rather than what was best for the team. They said my boy had no business starting at quarterback and that you, T.J. Farrell, were clearly the better player and should be the starter. Then they added, 'Or else.'"

"I . . ."

"They were probably correct," Coach interrupted me. "But that didn't make right those bastards interfering with my program."

"But Moose is dead."

"There are all kinds of dead," he snapped back at me.

I just wanted out. "I need to go," I said.

"Not yet. You accused me of being cold," Coach said and positioned himself between me and the door. "That meeting drained from me whatever sentimentality I had left regarding coaching football or this town."

"Why are you up here then? Why'd you come to Moose's vigil?" I asked.

"I didn't come for no vigil. I got a job to do. I'm sure you aren't aware of this, but if we win Friday, it'll be my two hundredth as a varsity football coach. That's a hall of fame number. I came up to figure out who's gonna replace Mooseburger on the offensive line. I'm leaning towards Scagnetti. What do you think?"

"You can't be serious," I said and tried to sidestep around him, but Coach mirrored my move with surprising quickness for a man in his late fifties.

"Serious as I can be. That two hundredth win and the hall of fame are pretty much all I have left to coach for. You see, I talked to my guy at Toledo. According to him, my name never came up yesterday — neither from you or Dr. Stone."

"I didn't have the chance, Coach. I spent most of the day with a grad assistant. I didn't think he would have much pull with Coach Markinson."

"I didn't expect you to work miracles, son. You're battling for their last scholarship. It's not like they were going to offer some sort of package deal including me just to land you. I just thought you could put in a good word, but apparently, that was too much to ask."

"Coach, I'm sorry."

"You're sorry are you? Let me tell you a little story."

"Coach, I really have to go."

"Trust me, someday you'll thank me for it. When I was a boy, one day I didn't take out the garbage like I was supposed to. My father got angry. He was a big man, you see, and not a very forgiving one. I said I was sorry, but he told me, 'Son, sorry doesn't feed the bulldog.' Well, we didn't have a bulldog, but his point was that I could say I was sorry until I was blue in the face, but the fact remained that I hadn't done what I'd been asked to do. The bulldog was still hungry, and the garbage was still stinking up the kitchen. He slipped off this thick, black leather belt he always wore and beat me right across the back of my thighs."

"So, what? Are you going to whip me, Coach?" I was growing tired of his bullshit.

"Not with a belt. No," he answered cryptically.

I stared him straight in the eyes. "Can I go now?"

Coach Harris didn't answer. He merely stepped out of the way and turned his shoulders to open up a path to the door.

When I exited the locker room, I found Caly brooding inside the idling Escalade. She was the only one remaining at the stadium. I walked sheepishly to the passenger side door and climbed in.

"I'm sorry. I just couldn't," I said.

She white-knuckled the leather-covered steering wheel with one hand at one o'clock and the other at eleven and stared straight ahead. I could tell that she was struggling to hold back a torrent of frustration and disappointment. "Let's just go. Everyone's already at the Tuckers' farm by now."

*****

Because northern Ohio is flat and hill-less – geographic features that foster low expectations for the present and even lower aspirations for the future – we could see the orange-red glow of the massive bonfire from at least a mile away. Brian Tucker lived with his grandfather in southern Erie County on Billings Road on over one hundred acres of farmland. Even by Goodness Falls standards, it was way out in the sticks. Brian's grandfather and Cory Morrison's father stood out in front of a wide culvert that had been constructed over the roadside drainage ditch to allow heavy machinery direct access into the fields from the road. They both waved flashlights with which they directed us onto the culvert then stopped us.

"One of you going to be the designated driver?" Mr. Tucker asked, alternately shining the light into our faces. Mr. Tucker was Brian's widower grandfather, and Brian was the orphaned accidental product of small town scandal. He had never known his migrant worker father, and his mother had abandoned him to his grandfather's care when Brian was just a baby.

"Yes," Caly answered. "I don't drink, Mr. Tucker, and T.J.'s in-season."

"Good for you, young lady. It's a terrible habit," he said then lifted his other hand to reveal a half-finished beer. Mr. Morrison laughed and returned his toast.

Most kids in Goodness Falls had their first beers long before they had their first kiss, especially the boys, many of whom grew up on farms or worked on them in the summers for up to fourteen hours a day. At the end of which it wasn't uncommon to be rewarded with a cold beer or two back in the barn – no matter what the age. The exceptions were the children of the relative newcomers like the Stones and their Willow Brook neighbors, who'd purchased large lots of former farmland cheaply and built humongous homes on them. These were mostly white-collared professionals who weren't raised in Goodness Falls, who worked outside of the community, who had never calloused their hands with a shovel or a rake, and who probably hadn't had a drink so pedestrian as a beer themselves since their last fraternity kegger.

"Follow the orange cones," Mr. Tucker said and pointed his flashlight beam into the field.

Caly did as instructed and soon we were backed up into and joined with the circle of vehicles, mostly pickups and jeeps, that stretched the circumference of the bonfire. But Caly was nervous. "What about the cops?"

"As long as nobody's drinking and driving, they'll be cool. Besides, they'll understand about Moose, and this is the first week of the playoffs. None of them want to be the prick who arrested a football player and got him suspended."

Kids were everywhere. Little puffs of expired breath and the lit end of cigars and cigarettes marked their locations and movements in the cool night air. A cacophony of music blared from car speakers as kids competed to capture the enormity of Moose's passing with just the right rock power ballad, country dirge, or rap valediction. I hadn't even reached the rear of the Escalade to pop the lift gate before someone handed me a beer.

"Are you going to drink that?" Caly asked. "You never drink during the season."

"I don't normally lose my best friend in a traffic accident either," I said, hoping the alcohol would at least temporarily numb what was becoming perpetual pain in my head.

"It's still a school night."

"I know it's a school night," I barked back. "I'll only have one or two. Look around. Most of these kids are drinking."

"Most of these kids are idiots," she correctly observed.

We opened the hatch of the Escalade, folded the rear seat down, and sat with our legs hanging out the back watching the fire blaze. Hours passed as kids stopped to share beers from their coolers and stories about Moose. What was strange was that every time someone began a recollection with "Remember the time . . .," I couldn't. It was like the stories were, at best, vaguely familiar although I'd been present at most of them. I didn't know it then, but memory loss is commonly experienced by CTE sufferers, and my memories were slow-leaking from my head like air from a balloon.

I lost track of the time and the count of how many beers I drank, but it was enough to diminish the pain and my usual inhibitions. At some point, I realized that the fire was dying and that there were only a few, widely-scattered vehicles remaining. Many were empty and left there by those who required rides home and would pick them up in the morning before school.

"Are you ready?" Caly asked.

"Not yet," I said, pulled her deeper into the Escalade, and closed the hatchback. Behind the tinted windows, we were invisible to the outside world.

"What are you doing?" Caly asked with a nervous laugh.

I didn't answer. I just lead with my tongue.

"Gross! You're drunk," Caly said, squished my cheeks between her thumb and forefinger, and turned my head away.

"And horny," I said and pulled her down so that we were lying side by side. My hand made repeated runs at the buttons on her blouse and the waistband of her yoga pants. "I want you so bad," I said pathetically and pressed myself hard against her.

"Really, T.J.? Shouldn't you be thinking about Moose?" Caly successfully fought off each advance.

"I am thinking about Moose." I rolled onto my back and paused in my advances. "I'm thinking that he died a virgin. I don't want to die a virgin." I unbuttoned and unzipped my jeans, rolled back onto my side, and tried once more to slip her pants down over her hips and butt.

Caly squirmed and resisted. "We talked about this. This isn't the way it's going to happen. At least not with me. You know that."

"I know," I said and backed off once again. "But that was before. Before Moose died and before I realized that it could have been me."

"What are you talking about? What could have been you?"

"The semi. It was only a few feet from my face when it swerved. Don't you see. It was supposed to be me dead not Moose. The license plate. Your father ..."

"You're drunk. You're not making any sense. What does my father have to do with anything?"

I grabbed her hand and forced it inside my pants. Caly only briefly squeezed it over my boxers like it was a stick of lit dynamite, then she balled her hand into a fist and refused to toss it.

"Damn it! You bitch!" I screamed, rolled onto my back, and slammed my fist against the rear side window.

Caly scampered away to the rear of the Escalade, where she rolled herself up into a frightened little ball.

"You tease me then you . . ." I couldn't finish my thought and much less my sentence, for the ceiling began to spin wildly. Before I could squeeze my way between and through the second row of leather, twin bucket seats to reach the handle for the back door, I was bent over and puking inside the Escalade.

From that point, I don't remember much, only the glow of an occasional streetlight passing overhead as I rode lying down in the back, freezing my ass off with the windows wide open, and then Caly opening up the hatchback and delivering me to the backdoor of my house, where my mom met me, led me up to my bedroom, and placed a metal bucket next to where my head lay throbbing on the bed in the whirlpool that my room and life had become.

Chapter Six

Monday, October, 29, 201_

I woke the next day in a complete fog. My head was pounding, my throat burned, and my abdominal muscles ached from the vomiting. Vague memories of the previous two days slowly crystallized: the accident, the recruiting visit, the vigil, the beer – the thought of which made my stomach retch. I picked up my phone from the night stand. Thirty-Seven texts! None were from Caly. Most were from teammates asking, "Dude, where are you?" Or commanding, "Get your ass to school." And, finally warning, "Coach is pissed!" One was from Coach Markinson at Toledo: "Looking forward to seeing you play Friday night. Bring your "A" game."

"School? Coach? What day is it," I thought. I looked at my phone once more and read, "11:36 A.M. Monday, October 29th." I threw my covers off, vaulted out of bed, and fell immediately to the floor as it spun beneath me.

My mom must have heard me fall, for in a matter of seconds, she was kneeling next to me and helping me back to my uncertain feet. "Oh, honey," she said. "You're too sick to go to school."

"I'm not sick, Mom. I'm drunk."

"Either way," she said clearly disappointed. "You need to get back in bed and get some sleep."

Still dressed in yesterday's clothes, I broke free and stumbled down the stairs into the kitchen. "Where're the keys to the truck?" I called behind me. "I need to get to school. If I don't go to school, I can't practice. If I don't practice, Coach will bench me. He's out to get me."

"Out to get you?" She questioned as she arrived in the kitchen. "Why would he be out to get you? You're the quarterback."

"It's nothing," I said. "Forget it." I totally regretted having said it. "Where are the truck keys?"

"Your dad took the truck to his job interview. Don't you remember?"

"Oh, Christ! What am I going to do?"

"I know what you're *not* going to do," she said. "You're not going to use the Lord's name in vain in my house, and you're not going to school like this. That would be worse. I've already called the school nurse and reported you sick. I'm sure Coach Harris will understand."

"What about Caly? Did she say anything when she dropped me off?"

"You were in such a state. There was no chance to talk."

"Oh, Mom. What have I done?" I said and sank into one of the kitchen chairs.

"Nothing that can't be fixed. You're a good boy. Coach Harris knows he needs you, and Caly knows she's lucky to have you. Now, let's get you back into bed."

"I need another pill, Mom. I won't be able to sleep without it."

"T.J. I don't think it's a good idea to . . ."

"I NEED IT!" I snapped.

Clearly frightened by my anger, she relented, went into the bathroom, and returned with my temporary escape from the pain and my stupidity.

Before I passed out once again, I texted Caly several times, but she was either unable to or refusing to respond. When I woke up, it was nearly five o'clock. My father had returned. I showered, dressed, then grabbed the keys to the Ranger. I yelled, "I'm taking the truck. I won't be long," then hurried from the house to avoid any protest or further discussion.

I pulled into the stadium parking lot and parked the truck just as the team was exiting the field. With daylight savings time in effect, darkness had descended precipitously. In order to extend practice time and ensure optimal conditions during the temperamental weather patterns of Ohio's autumn, Coach moved practices from the grass practice field next to the stadium to the game field with its state-of-the-art synthetic turf and lighting. What pissed me off was that it looked like the end of any Monday practice, as if two days earlier we hadn't lost a teammate and friend, and in two more days, we wouldn't be lowering him into the ground.

Determined to steer directly into the impending storm and move on as quickly as possible, I worked my way against the flow of my teammates as they dragged themselves towards the locker room with steam literally rising from their scalps. Like an ascendant Caesar, red-haired Pete Terwilliger led the exodus. Pete's family lived in Willow Brook and socialized with the Stones. He and Caly even dated for a while before she and I became a couple. Throughout grade school, he was our classmate, but his ultracompetitive father demanded Pete be held back for a second year of the eighth grade, knowing Pete would probably never beat me out and to give him another year's growth before entering high school. It's what people in Goodness Falls called a "redneck redshirt." He was the back-up quarterback and my heir apparent. Terwilliger gave me a cocky backwards nod of recognition that reeked of teenage cool and one-upmanship. I swear I wanted to punch him in the face.

"Nice that you could join us, superstar," someone said from inside the phalanx.

"Asshole," was the angry reaction to my late arrival from another one of the helmeted Ducks.

"Getting your shillelagh spit polished, Farrell?" Another added, sparking a chorus of grunts and groans.

I recognized the voice, "Very funny, Morrison. Can you even spell shillelagh?"

"Coach made us run extra for you missing practice. Thanks a lot, dickhead. I can spell that: T – period – J – period."

A pack of assistant coaches rode herd behind the players. Each of them, including Coach McKuen, my quarterback coach, cast looks of disappointment at me as if I'd delivered our game plan to the Lakeview Pirates rather than simply missed a Monday night football practice. Excessive or not, I knew the code. I had lived it for the past eight years without violation. I would have responded in the exact manner as my teammates and coaches. There was a penance to be paid.

I spotted Coach Harris standing near the thirty-yard line, making post-practice notes on his clipboard.

Stepping from the sidelines onto the playing field, I called out to him through a puff of breath. I hoped to steal a look at Coach's face and make a preemptive read of just how deep I was in his doghouse. Coach Harris, however, remained back turned, ignoring me. He had experienced many such showdowns with teenage boys. He was not going to be suckered into making the first move.

"Coach Harris," I said once more when I was within five yards.

This time, Coach slowly turned about and looked me up and down then down and up. "Well, well. Look who decided to come to practice. Decide to take the day off Farrell? Or what?"

"No, sir." I was determined to humble myself to whatever degree necessary.

"So. What? Were you too overcome with grieving to practice?" His voice betrayed his rising irritation.

I ignored his incredible callousness. "I'm sorry, sir," I answered, figuring my best strategy was to get to the apology as soon as possible, but Coach Harris was in no mood to grant a merciful end to my torture.

"Sorry? You're sorry? You're like a broken record with all of your sorrys, Farrell."

"Yes, sir."

"We're about to enter the state playoffs. Your teammates are out here busting their asses while you're what? Home with the flu? This is football season, son. Not flu season. He stepped forward so that his nose was no more than six inches from mine. "Or were you still hung over?"

I could barely see through the constant flow of his exhaled breaths to read his expression, but he clearly saw the fear in mine.

"Did you really think I wouldn't find out? This is Goodness Falls for God's sake. If someone farts on one side of town, they smell it on the other."

"I . . . um . . . I . . . um." He had me and I didn't know how to respond.

"As much as I'd like to, I'm not kicking you off the team, Farrell. I'd have to get rid of the entire senior class. I'll play dumb. But at least the rest of the senior class showed up for work today. Where were you? We went over the game plan for Lakeview," Coach continued, "and you missed the entire session."

"We've played them before, Coach, and I'll get inside my scouting report extra deep. I promise."

"That's all well and good, Farrell, but as of this moment, Terwilliger is my starting quarterback."

"But . . ."

"But nothing. And this time, I don't give a damn what Dr. Stone and those boosters think or say."

I heard all he said, but I was focused on ". . . *as of this moment*, Terwilliger is my starting quarterback." Coach Harris had left himself an out. He knew – better than most – my importance to the team. I was confident that by the week's end, he would find a way to justify my reinsertion into the lineup.

"Yes, sir. I understand," I said, then I turned toward the locker room in order to begin repairing the damage I'd done to my reputation with my teammates – who knew best–what I meant to their chances of success.

"Where you think you're going, Farrell?"

I looked back confused.

"On the line," Coach said.

"The line?"

"You owe me a few Duck Reminders."

"Now, Coach?"

"Now! On the line!"

I jogged towards the near goal line, but not having expected to work out, I'd worn my typical button down flannel shirt, blue jeans, and work boots, which was far from the appropriate workout gear. I turned to face Coach.

"On the whistle!" Coach yelled. A shrill blare sounded and I took off running. With each step, my feet slid inside the boots, and my heel lifted and chafed against the hard back. The height of the boots exerted unusual stress on my shins, and I knew immediately I'd suffer from shin splints in the morning.

A second whistle prompted me to dive to the abrasive turf, do five push-ups, pull myself to my feet, and resume the sprint. A third whistle sent me to the ground again and back into push-up mode. The pattern continued for a full one-hundred yards.

"Again!" Coach yelled, having repositioned himself at the fifty yard line and "Again," when I'd reached my original starting point.

I lost track of time. My vision grew blurry and my head pounded as the initial symptoms of dehydration checked in. A distant ringing began in my left ear and steadily rose in pitch. Pressure, more and more pressure, pressed over my ear and threatened to blow a hole in the side of my head from the inside out. But, I kept on running. The remaining alcohol in my system steamed from my pores and sweat soaked through my un-tucked shirt. Steam rose from my scalp and dissipated into the night air. The back of my heel was soon rubbed raw and bloody. I kicked off my boots and continued in my stocking feet. Each wintergreen breath burned my lungs.

I was semi-conscious of my teammates filtering out of the locker room in singles and sets. Occasionally, one would turn in my direction and shake his head before continuing on his way. Later, the assistant coaches emerged, climbed into their vehicles, and drove out through the chain link gate. The whistles continued until my sprint was barely a jog, and I was doing ladies' pushups from my knees.

Finally, Coach Harris yelled, "Take it in," and he abandoned the field.

I collapsed face first in the end zone and lay exhausted and delirious for I'm not sure how long before a pair of dirt-covered, steel-toed work boots at the end of two tree-stump sized calves appeared before my ant's-eye view. I was unable to lift my head to see beyond my visitor's knee-caps.

"*Carpe Diem,* motherfucker!"

It was Moose! As large and alive as ever.

"Moose," I said with surprising calm, "I am so glad to see you. I am so glad that you're not . . ."

"Dead?" He finished my sentence.

"Yeah. That." Exhausted, I closed my eyes. "I tried to get that asshole to stop, to go and help. But he just drove away. If it wasn't for him, you and I'd have gone duck hunting like we'd planned, and you wouldn't have . . ."

"Died?" He finished my sentence once more.

And once more I said, "Yeah. That."

The mist from earlier had given way to a thickening fog. A loud "kachunk" accompanied the sudden shut off of the stadium lights, which turned the world to pitch. I rolled onto my back and looked up, but Moose was gone.

"I miss you, Moose. I'm sorry!" I screamed towards the heavens. "It should have been me."

*****

It was nearly eight o'clock by the time I coaxed myself out of the shower and toweled off. My clothes were all but ruined and stinky, so I dressed in a matching set of gray Fighting Ducks Football sweat pants and a hooded sweatshirt that I pulled from the bottom of my locker. I had yet to fully recover from Friday's game night beating and even much less the one just administered by Coach Harris. I wanted nothing more than to go home, eat a hot meal, take another Vicodin, climb into bed, and start over the next day, but my evening of damage control was just beginning. And I sensed that it was going to get worse.

Driving to Caly's, I scrolled through my messages and missed calls. None were from her.

I had paid a heavy price for missing practice, but I felt that I had football under control. Yeah, Coach had given my position to Terwilliger, but Monday was a light day of practice: no contact and everything done at half speed. Anyone can play like an All-American under those conditions. Wednesday's practice was always the test, when, for the last fifteen minutes, the number one offensive unit scrimmaged the number one defensive unit under game conditions: full contact, full speed. Except for mop up duty, Terwilliger hadn't even taken a varsity snap. Until Wednesday, I would play Coach's whipping boy and bide my time. Let Terwilliger prove himself then.

Caly, however, was a different story. And all of a sudden, mine and my family's future was riding on me patching up the holes I'd punctured in our relationship.

*****

Caly's mother answered my ring of the doorbell. Mr. Stone stood slightly behind, peering over his wife's left shoulder and creating the illusion of a mythological two-headed monster.

"Is Caly home?" I asked as if I hadn't projectile vomited the previous evening inside their brand new, hundred thousand dollar vehicle.

Mrs. Stone's stare flung imaginary daggers. Silently, she debated her options while I squirmed.

"Hello, T.J.," Mr. Stone answered, swallowing his own anger for the obvious reason that his own security depended on my continued silence regarding the accident and the damaged Benz, which meant that I had him by the balls. "I'm not sure that Caly is in the mood for a visitor tonight."

"I'm right here, Daddy," Caly said from behind them. "Let him in."

I was forced to shuffle around Mrs. Stone, who stood Medusa-like, still staring and still considering her best course of action.

"We'll be down the basement," Caly said before curtly turning, opening the door, and descending the stairs that entered the floor-to-second-story-ceiling foyer just prior to the massive kitchen in the back of the house with its marble counter tops and stainless steel appliances. Like me, Ally was an only child, but the Stones' kitchen was fitted and sized for a Goodness Falls, Ohio, season of *The Real World*. The basement was my and Ally's sanctuary from her parents, where we went to watch TV and hang out.

I left the basement door open, as was the rule, and nervously descended the wooden stairs. A lifetime spent in the football culture had well-prepared me for Coach Harris's tirade, but I had fewer than two years of experience in the mysterious world of boyfriends and girlfriends; therefore, I was in no hurry to discover the horrors that waited for me below.

Caly sat cross-legged and cross-armed on a massive, L-shaped, brown corduroy couch. Her natural blond hair was pulled back, restrained by a wide, pink headband. The 62-inch LCD television was tuned to some inane reality program on MTV, which Caly loved and I hated, about privileged and annoyingly pretentious sons and daughters of celebrities. But she couldn't really watch it through the tears that had already pooled in her green eyes then spilled onto the cliffs of her ridiculously high cheekbones before gathering until sufficient to form a cataract and fall down her face.

My instinct was to apply the same get-it-over-with strategy that I employed with Coach, so I cut to the apology. "I'm really sorry about last night. I didn't mean it. I lost control. That wasn't me."

Caly unfolded herself in a spasm of anger and catapulted to the edge of the couch cushion with her feet planted on the floor and her hands balled up in fists at her sides. "My father had to take the Escalade in for detailing. It's going to cost over three hundred dollars. My parents are so pissed! They've grounded me from driving except to school and cheer practice."

I walked around the corner of the couch and stood facing her.

"I didn't even know you last night," she said. "I know you were upset, but that doesn't give you the right to be a total jerk. What I've always loved about you, T.J., is that you're not like other guys. Please, don't ever do that again."

"I won't. I promise. But I have to tell you that Moose's dying has made me re-think some things."

"No. Don't re-think anything. Don't mess this up." She wagged her finger back and forth to indicate that by "this" she meant the two of us as a couple.

"But what happened to Moose. It could happen to anybody. And, like, there's really no such thing as the future, only the present. And if you want to do stuff, you better do it now."

"Wow, that's soooo deep."

"Don't make fun," I insisted. "I'm being serious."

"Are you? I think you're just looking for more excuses to try and get inside my pants."

"Look," I said. "Just forgive me. Let's get through this week, and we can talk about it later."

Caly didn't provide the reassurance I so desperately sought. It was still too soon. "You know what?" She said. "I think my mom's right. You should just go."

"Caly," I said, stretching the pronunciation of her name into five syllables in the pleading manner of children. "I saw Moose."

The look Caly gave me was the exact replica of her mother's death stare.

"I talked to him," I said.

"You mean like in a dream?"

"No. I was wide awake. At the stadium."

"Are you still drunk?"

"No. I'm serious. He looked as real as you do."

"You mean like a ghost?"

"I don't know."

Caly tried to process my claim. "You're talking crazy," she concluded.

"I'm not crazy. I saw him. I swear. I talked to him."

"You definitely should go," she said and abruptly jumped up from the couch, covered her face, ran up the stairs, and left me sitting alone.

I turned off the television, and wary of the possibility of an ambush by Mrs. Stone at the top of the stairs, I cautiously climbed out of the basement. Halfway up, my head began to spin in a vertiginous whirl. Every muscle in my body rebelled against its activation. A stitch stabbed at my left side, and both calves cramped and forced me to sit and to rub them out.

When I finally reached the ground floor, I was met by Dr. Stone. Apparently, Mrs. Stone was upstairs comforting Caly. Out of his wife's presence, Dr. Stone didn't seem quite so dismayed by the last two day's events. He was being what he had described to me last Friday as his practical self.

He tried to put his arm around my shoulders, but I shrugged it off. He escorted me out the front door, across the front lawn, and towards the pickup in the driveway. "You need to get your shit together, young man. You're falling apart on me. I thought we had an understanding. I thought we were a team."

"I'm not on your team."

"That's funny. Because Chief Johnson stopped by earlier and said he had run into you at the hospital, which – by the way – was very stupid. He said he spoke to you about Saturday morning and that you'd said you hadn't seen anything unusual. I corroborated your story. All of which made me think that we *were* on the same team."

"I know what I said, but it's not the truth." A blinding white lightning bolt flashed behind my eyeballs. The fucking migraine had returned.

"The truth? The truth?" Dr. Stone said. "The truth is whatever *we* say it is, and the truth is you'll screw up a lot of lives if you don't stick to the story we've agreed upon." Inside my scrambled head, his voice sounded as if we were having the conversation under water, but even through the garbled words, his tone clearly indicated that his patience with me had worn thin. "It's time for you to grow up. This isn't a game we're playing here. We could both lose everything." He softened his tone a little. "What you need to do now is get refocused on football. Nothing would help everyone heal faster and move past all of this than a deep run into the playoffs."

"You've got to be kidding me," I said, then climbed inside the pickup and backed away over a puddle of oil the truck's engine had bled onto the driveway.

Chapter Seven

Tuesday Afternoon, October 30, 201_

School was more of a hell than usual. My goal for the day was to go cold turkey on the Vicodin, clear my head, and to start winning my job back at practice. However, between my dread over having to attend Moose's wake at the funeral home later that evening and the jackhammer relentlessly chipping away at my skull, I couldn't concentrate on a single word my teachers said. Because Caly was in all honors courses and I wasn't in any, she managed to avoid me all day.

On Monday, while I had stayed home hung over, the school had been overrun by grief counselors and local pastors at the disposal of grieving students, but they were gone already.

Change the station.

Close the App.

Ctrl-Alt-Del.

In what I know now was my still-concussed state, my attention span had been whittled down to nearly nothing. The only thing that stuck with me from that entire school day was Mr. Mortis, the substitute English teacher, reading from Shakespeare's *Macbeth* as part of Senior English, Unit 2: Tragedy.

He was dressed entirely in black: black motorcycle boots, black jeans, and a black button-down shirt open at the sleeves and at the neck to reveal a heavy silver chain and Celtic cross. He wore his jet black hair in a sort of punked-out style, and his fingernails were painted a deep purple. All of which rendered him a little more than conspicuous at Goodness Falls High School. I couldn't imagine how shallow the school district's substitute teacher pool must have been for Mr. Mortis to get the gig.

Some kids had Googled him and found that he played lead guitar in an underground death metal band called Yorick. Their evidence was a blurry picture of some shirtless dude in black leather pants leaning back in full rocker pose and thrashing an electric guitar. They'd found and printed it off of the Internet. I couldn't say it was definitely Mr. Mortis, but the cross around the guitar player's neck in the picture matched the one Mr. Mortis wore. All I know is that he had never substituted in the school before that week.

Mr. Mortis recited from Act V, Scene v of *Macbeth*:

And all our yesterdays have lighted fools
The way to dusty death. Out, out, brief candle!
Life's but a walking shadow, a poor player
That struts and frets his hour upon the stage
And then is heard no more. It is a tale
Told by an idiot, full of sound and fury,
Signifying nothing.

"I love that soliloquy," Mr. Mortis said with actual tears welling in his eyes and mixing with a micro-thin line of black mascara.

Expecting them to share my dismay at Mr. Mortis' insensitive choice of material on the day many of us would attend a wake for our classmate, I looked around the room for signs of shared outrage. However, no one else seemed the least bit bothered. I hated them for their apparent indifference. Actually, no one else even seemed entirely conscious. Most of my classmates wore the same glassy-eyed expression of total boredom that they wore on every school day.

"What are you going to do?" Moose whispered from the previously empty seat to my left.

"Moose?!" I turned back around and whispered-screamed. The skin was peeled back on his forehead, revealing pinkish flesh and ivory-colored skull. His nose was broken and off center. His eyes were blackened and bloody and he was missing most of his teeth.

"T.J.?" Mr. Mortis excitedly called on me. "Do you have a question or comment?"

I looked to him but didn't respond. When I turned my attention back to Moose's seat, he was gone.

"T.J.?" Mr. Mortis repeated.

"No," I said and left him disappointed.

Clearly familiar with the zombie expressions on the faces seated in front of him, Mr. Mortis held a fist in front of his mouth like a microphone, pounded it with his other hand, and in the deadpan voice of a bombing stand-up comedian, he joked, "I'll be here all week."

The bell rang to end the period and the school day. Lazarus-like, the lifeless bodies of my fellow students miraculously reinvigorated. They sprang from their desks with their phones reignited and all but sprinted out the door and into the already fast-flowing stream of students flooding the hallway.

Once the classroom had emptied and I'd gathered my wits, I approached Mr. Mortis where he stood behind a podium. "Mr. Mortis, you're a substitute and this is a small town, so I know you don't live here. Maybe you don't know that a student died in an accident last Saturday."

"I do know. It was David Mooseburger. He sits right there," he pointed to Moose's empty desk.

My irrational first thought had been that Mr. Mortis had also seen the ghost of Moose. "How did you know that?"

He held up a laminated seating chart.

"If you knew about Moose, I'm surprised that you'd read that crap from Shakespeare? It's all about death."

"I'm not sure I'd call much of Shakespeare 'crap,' but I'm glad you were paying attention."

"Why'd you read it? Couldn't you have put it off for another day or two?"

"I could have, but I don't like to be 'put off.' There's a plan and it's my job to execute it. Besides, one should never be surprised by death. Angry? Sure. Sad? Why not? But never surprised."

"It just seemed insensitive. That's all I'm saying."

"First off, Mr. Miller's instructions indicated that the class has been studying Shakespearean tragedy. Secondly, why not? Should we not read *Huckleberry Finn* if someone in the class is African-American? Should we not read Dickens if someone in the class is poor? Should we skip Whitman entirely because someone may be gay? And thirdly, those lines from *Macbeth* aren't about death. They're about life. Read them again." Mr. Mortis looked over my shoulder at the clock on the back wall. "Was there anything else, T.J.? I have a four o'clock in Toledo."

A 'four o'clock' what? I wondered, but "No," is how I answered.

*****

My day didn't much improve after school. In addition to dealing with what felt like a spike being driven – tap-by-agonizing-tap – into the side of my skull, I received a collective cold shoulder pad at practice. My teammates clearly had yet to forgive me for the extra conditioning they'd received the day before or for my lack of focus on playoff preparation. Inside his newly-assigned red scrimmage jersey reserved for the starting quarterback, Terwilliger preened like a prize rooster among his junior teammates on the opposite side of the locker room. On a football practice field, a red jersey marked its wearer as untouchable by the other players.

I stood in front of my stall strapping on my shoulder pads. Moose's locker had been cleaned out and his personal effects boxed up for his family, but his game jersey was draped over the front as some sort of cheesy motivation for the rest of us. For similar purposes, a black #54 decal had been added to everyone's helmet. One of the student trainers had swapped out my fractured concussion-proof helmet with a new but regular one. I watched the typical locker room antics I'd seen and participated in hundreds of times myself, but it all seemed childish and stupid.

"What the hell's the matter with you, Farrell?" Cory Morrison snuck up in front of me and said, accompanied by a two-handed shiver to the breastplate of my shoulder pads. "You're a piss poor captain, skipping practice and getting everybody else extra conditioning." Morrison was every bit as good a football player as me, maybe better. He was, however, too short, too light, and two-tenths of a second too slow in the forty yard dash to attract the attention of division one colleges.

I stumbled backward, caught myself, then stepped right back into Morrison's grill. "What's the matter with me, asshole, is that you're full of shit. You always have been and I'm tired of it." I returned his shove, and if not for his buddy, Danny Sorenstam, standing directly behind him, Morrison would have toppled onto his ass.

With a nudge from Sorenstam, Morrison was right back in my face, "You want to go, pretty boy?"

"What's going on out here?" Coach Harris interrupted, emerging from the office.

"Nothing, Coach. Just having a little talk with the *backup* quarterback. That's all," Morrison said, continuing the stare down.

Coach Harris wasn't stupid. He'd spent most of his life inside locker rooms. A little piss and vinegar was good for a football team, and he loved the overachieving Cory Morrisons of the world.

"Get these guys to the practice field, Cory. We're burning daylight," Coach said.

"Yes, sir," Morrison said. When he turned away from me, he made sure the right flap of his shoulder pad contacted my chest enough to brush me back. "Saddle up, fellas," Morrison called, and like simpleminded cowpokes they followed him out of the locker room.

With my jersey in hand, I headed for the door, but Coach Harris called me back. "Got a present for you, Farrell." He tossed me a white scrimmage jersey like those worn by the rest of the players. Wearing it would remove the bubble of invincibility to which I'd grown accustomed. Outside of Wednesday's fifteen minutes of full contact, I hadn't been hit by a teammate since the beginning of my junior year.

"Are you serious?"

Harris was immediately in my face. "Are you questioning my decisions, son? Are you the coach of this football team? Cause if you are, I didn't get that memo. And until I do, you answer to me. *You* do as *I* say. Is that clear?" Coach pushed and prodded. "If you can't play according to my rules, there's the door." He pointed over my shoulder.

For just a moment, I let loose the devil inside. "I'm not your 'son,' and it wasn't my fault, Coach." I'd been wanting to say that for over a year. It felt good.

"Not my fault? What are you talking about Farrell?"

"Nothing," I retreated.

"No, Farrell. Step up. Tell me. What exactly wasn't my fault?"

"You know what I'm talking about."

"No, Farrell. I don't. Enlighten me."

"Your son. It's not my fault that you benched Donny last year. And his . . ."

"His what?"

"His . . . his . . . you know . . . the people he's hanging around with now . . . what he's doing . . . you know what I mean. That's not my fault either."

Coach's face turned so red I thought it might explode, but he swallowed it instead. He stared deeper into my eyes than anyone ever had. I watched as arteries surfaced and shot like red streaks of heat lightning across the whites of his eyes. Finally, he said, "That's enough, Farrell. Hit the field."

I turned toward the door.

"And, Farrell. You keep your head on a swivel out there. You're not wearing this red dress anymore." He ripped my red jersey from my hand and flung it towards a manager, who collected it from off the floor and returned it to the equipment room. "Do you have anything else to say, Farrell?"

"No, sir."

"Then get that white jersey on and get out to practice."

I slipped the mesh jersey over my pads and exited the locker room.

Anthony Scagnetti was still outside adjusting his equipment. Scags was a thirteen-year classmate of mine. His dad had been a meat cutter at the plant when my dad worked there. We were never close friends but we always ran in the same academic, athletic, and social circles. Built short, squat, and chesty like a bulldog and possessing the same disposition, Scags was also Moose's back up and would be taking his spot in the starting line-up. He looked at me oddly and asked, "What the hell are you wearing?"

"Coach gave it to me. I think he's testing me."

"Testing you? Hell, he's going to get you killed. Some of those guys will be drooling all over themselves when they see you out of the red. You might want to remind Coach about that scholarship you're sucking so much dick for."

"Don't worry about me, Moose. I can take care of myself."

"Moose?" Scagnetti scrunched his face and asked.

"What?"

"You called me 'Moose.'"

"I did?"

I looked away and rubbed the back of my neck distractedly. Scagsie placed his hand up on my shoulder.

"Is everything alright?" He asked. "You ain't been yourself. I mean, you missed practice yesterday, dude. When's the last time Touchdown T.J. Farrell missed a football practice?"

"Never."

"Right. Maybe you need some more time. Take another day off."

"Can't. I've got to play Friday. Toledo's coach is coming to see me play, and right now, I'm not even starting."

"Terwilliger?"

I nodded.

"He's such a douche. You want me to take him out or something?"

"No. I got it."

"You sure? You know I will."

"Positive. Let's go before we're late for stretching and Coach kicks both our asses."

*****

Other than my replacement helmet feeling as if it weighed a hundred pounds, it was a typical Tuesday. Coach Harris ran militaristic practices timed to the minute with no variations. Except for the ear-splitting sounds of whistles blowing, pads popping, coaches yelling, and bullhorns blaring, the routine and predictability of it all comforted me.

I was awkwardly partnered with Terwilliger during throwing drills, but I gritted my teeth and swallowed my pride. During the seven-on-seven passing session, Coach McKuen gave me a few reps with the first team. "Just in case," he told me. In an odd way, I enjoyed having the pressure of expectation, leadership, and execution removed from my shoulders and placed on someone else's for a change. I even enjoyed seeing Terwilliger a little stressed by his inherited burden. The vacation ended, however, when the blast from the bullhorn signaled the beginning of the "team defense" session.

"Farrell!" Coach Harris called. "Quarterback." He used it as a verb.

A stunned silence of disbelief fell over the practice field. I'd never taken part in the team defense period. It had always been my time to work independently on position and game-specific skills and reads.

The silence was broken by Morrison's bloodthirsty wolf's howl. He was the starting inside linebacker for the Ducks' defense, which made him the only two-way player on the entire team. "Fresh meat!" Morrison shouted.

I was being ordered to run the scout team offense, manned by a bunch of underdeveloped sophomores, who typically only played junior varsity. Hell, even the more-promising sophomores were spared from this humiliation and torture for fear of injury. Ostensibly, the scout team was charged with the responsibility of mimicking the offense of that particular week's opponent, but in reality, they were sacrificial lambs, the outlet onto which the first team upperclassmen vented their aggression in coach-controlled bursts until game night, when the entire avalanche of their carefully-managed rage could be unleashed. The coaches called it the "scout team;" the players called it the "Goon Squad." I had never played with the Goonies; I had always been shielded from that suicide mission.

I tried not to betray my surprise – or fear – and jogged into the Goon Squad huddle. The sophomores looked at me as if I were some kind of long-awaited messiah. I felt ashamed that I couldn't identify a single one by name.

Coach McKuen called the plays for the Goon Squad. He'd hold up a card with a play from the opponent's playbook diagrammed on it, and the Goonies would attempt to execute their assignments as drawn. In reality, as soon as the ball was snapped, they cowered, ducked, and covered.

"I've got the whistle," Coach Harris informed the rest of the coaching staff, meaning only he could bring a play to an end and, thereby, call off the dogs.

The first play called was a simple isolation play, which required me to do no more than hand the ball off to the tailback then to bootleg away from the theoretical hole. Sliding the back of my right hand between the legs and against the sophomore center's crotch felt strange and oddly inappropriate – a little like cheating. Moose had been my center since pee wee football. My hands could snuggle into their position against Moose's ample rear end on their own.

As the first team middle linebacker, Morrison was lined up directly over me and my scared shitless center at about a four yards depth. Considering where my hands were, my center's shitlessness was probably a good thing. A malicious smile exposed Morrison's black mouthpiece. "You're mine, bitch," he said. "No pretty red jersey is going to protect your ass today, faggot."

I tried to ignore him and call out the signals. Thinking Morrison's threats were directed at him, the center, not privy to the social politics of the senior class, shook with fear. When I called, "Hut," the poor kid hit the ground so fast that the snap never made it to my hands. Instinctively, I and every defensive player near the fumble dove for the ball. A pile formed in which I was nearly castrated by a vicious nut grab – a fairly common cheap shot at the bottom of football piles but not usually deployed against a teammate in practice. In the chaos of the melee, I couldn't identify my assailant, but I safely assumed it to be Morrison, who was notorious for his testicle twists. Coaches peeled the players off the pile one by one. The only Goonies untangled were me and my center. The rest had gladly conceded the possession of the ball and immediately returned to the huddle.

"Run it again!" Coach McKuen ordered.

Despite similar threats from Morrison, this time the snap made it into my hands. I delivered the ball deep in the backfield to the tailback then peeled away and carried out an innocuous bootleg fake. My nonchalance was met by the top of a helmet exploding up and through my chin. Morrison had ignored his reads and gap responsibilities. Instead, he took a direct route to me and delivered a highlight reel hit that gashed my chin wide open.

A collective "Ooooooh!" rose from players and coaches alike as my ass landed first then the back of my helmet-heavy head whiplashed against the ground. I thought, for sure, I'd fractured another helmet and possibly my skull.

"Blood in the water!" Morrison screamed standing menacingly over my crumpled form.

"Huddle up," the defensive coaches yelled.

Schultzie came immediately to my aid. I lay trying to stop the ringing in my ears, rubbing my chin, and wiping the blood off of my hand and onto my white practice pants.

"Let me look at that," Schultzie said. He undid my chinstrap and said, "You might need a few stitches." From his crouch, he turned to Coach McKuen, "You need a new QB, Coach."

"No!" I insisted. "I'm fine. I'm not coming out. Put a band aid on it."

"T.J.," Schultzie began, "this could get . . ."

"You heard him. Put a band aid on it," Coach Harris ordered.

After patching my spliced chin with a three-inch wide band aid, Schultzie placed his hand in front of my face mask and asked, "What day is it?"

I took a shot. "Tuesday," I said with as much feigned certainty as I could muster. Remarkably, I was correct.

"How many fingers do I have up?"

"Two," I answered because it's always two. I must have been right again, for he helped me to my feet and reluctantly allowed me to continue. I dragged myself back into my huddle of vestal virgins. They looked at the seeping, red band aid of courage on my chin with awe paired with confusion. In their minds that cut was a one-way ticket out of the Goon Squad huddle and to behind-the-lines safety. If played right, it could even have been stretched to a day off of practice the next day.

My newly-intimate center gathered the courage to speak, "Are you all right, man?"

"I'm good, but could you guys at least *try* to slow them down a little?"

No one responded. Knowing the unlikelihood of that happening, they didn't want to encourage me by providing false hope.

For the next play, Coach McKuen mercifully called a simple toss sweep that should have theoretically kept me out of harm's way and Morrison's, but he was in no mood for mercy. As soon as the backside guard pulled behind the center, Morrison should have followed him to the ball carrier; instead, he tore through the gap and lit me up from behind. Paying no attention whatsoever to the ball carrier, he planted his face mask in the small of my back beneath my rib pads and drove me face first into the turf. Morrison gave me a little shove as I started to rise, "Stay down, bitch," he said.

Once again, I staggered back to the huddle then cringed when Coach McKuen held up the next play, a pass, which meant the entire defensive line would be bearing down on me.

Spying behind the huddle, Coach Harris saw the diagram of the pass play, smiled around the metal whistle clinched between his yellowed teeth, and signaled to the defensive coordinator that he wanted a delayed inside blitz, meaning Morrison would be let loose to rush me after feigning a pass drop.

"Get rid of it quickly," Coach McKuen advised me.

The shotgun snap was high. By the time I pulled it down to locate my receivers, I was looking into a wall of onrushing tacklers. They collectively recognized the gratuitousness of delivering such a cheap shot on a teammate. They pulled up. Morrison arrived a beat later, just as I relaxed in appreciation of the sportsmanship shown by the defensive linemen. I was completely off guard. As Morrison's helmet collided with my breastplate, my head snapped violently forward then back in a whip-like manner. I felt as if I had been broken in half and decapitated as I writhed breathlessly on the turf. For a moment, I thought I was going to die.

Once again, Schultzie hurried to my side. "Deep breaths, T.J. Deep breaths. You got the wind knocked out of you. I want you to take a few plays off."

"No! I gasped and gritted my teeth against the pain.

"T.J.," Schultzie whispered, "this ain't no goddamn *Rocky* movie. You're going get yourself killed."

"This is bullshit," Scagnetti complained to no one in particular, then marched into the Goon Squad huddle and replaced the grateful center, who experienced a come-to-Jesus moment.

"Scagsie," Coach McKuen started, "you can't . . ."

"I'm playing, Coach. If I don't, he's gonna get killed."

I watched as McKuen looked for a cue from Coach Harris, who appeared to appreciate the new card put in play and nodded his approval.

Rising to my feet, I exchanged an appreciative look with Scags. The rest of the Goonies seemed somehow invigorated and flushed with confidence by the presence of two varsity starters in their huddle. In a voice a full octave removed from puberty, one even exhorted, "Let's do this!"

"You heard the man," I managed to say though still short of breath.

Caught up in the spirit of the Goonie uprising, Coach McKuen held up an inside zone play, which called for a double team block on Morrison by the center and guard.

At the line of scrimmage, Scags glared across at Morrison. "Let's see what you got now, douche bag."

"Bring it on, fat boy," Morrison growled.

With Scags at center, I felt protected and reinvigorated. I called the signals and handed the ball to the tailback, who shockingly found an opening resembling a hole through which to run. Scags and his partner had driven Morrison five yards downfield and pancake-blocked his ass. We Goonies actually gained seven yards.

Coach Harris immediately tore into an expletive-laced tirade directed at his defensive players and coaches. But the Goonies were inspired. We sprinted back to the huddle cheering, exchanging fist bumps, and actually looking forward to the next play and another opportunity to embarrass the defense.

Coach McKuen fed off our enthusiasm and strategically called for a screen pass that would take advantage of the defense's over-exuberance to make up for having been beaten on the previous play. My Goonie linemen executed it to perfection by allowing the rushers to infiltrate the backfield before they stalk blocked the linebackers downfield. I drew the defensive lineman to me like mice to the cheese, then deftly dumped the ball over their heads and into the waiting arms of the tailback, who got into the hip pockets of his linemen and broke the play for a score.

I ran the length of the field to celebrate with the other Goonies. I swear that it was the most joy I had ever felt in a football uniform. But my glee was short-lived and the victory was Pyrrhic. We Goonies had violated one of the many unspoken codes of football players everywhere: "Thou shalt not show up the first team!" There was hell to pay. After another verbal beat down by Coach Harris, the defense was chomping on their mouthpieces, hungry for revenge.

"Scags! That's enough. Get out of there. What do you think you're doing?" Coach Harris yelled.

Scags gave me a hangdog look. "Sorry, man."

"Not your problem, Moose. Thanks."

Scags paused as if he intended to correct me once again. Instead, he turned to Schultzie. "You need to get him out of there."

Schultzie threw up his powerless hands.

The rest of the scrimmage session was a massacre. Each attempt at a play was blown up by the inspired defense. I was repeatedly drilled and thrown to the ground. The whistle to end the plays grew increasingly tardy, so that late and unnecessary hits were delivered with regularity and impunity. I didn't complain because on some level I felt like I deserved it – you know, for Moose's death and its cover up – however, even the assistant coaches began looking to one another and helplessly reaching for – but not blowing – their own whistles, desiring to put an end to the bloodbath.

After twenty-five minutes, the pummeling was finally brought to an end. Coach Harris called the players into a one-kneed semi-circle and preached on toughness, loyalty, and team. He finished by calling on Terwilliger to lead the team in its customary post-practice "Our Father."

I refused even to mouth the words. Instead, I stared spitefully into Coach Harris's self-satisfied eyes.

*****

I was last into the showers, which consisted of three separate stalls, separated by chest high concrete block walls. Each contained a centered pole with six shower heads equidistantly spaced around it. I stood alone with my head bowed in pain under the shower in the middle stall and slowly turned the handle so that the water temperature inched ever closer to scalding. The cascading water and the steam rising from the concrete floor permeated the space and hid my tears.

"Don't be such a pussy, T-bag," a voice cut through the steam and the noise of the pounding spray. Only Moose called me "T-bag." He called me it because he knew I hated it.

I backed hurriedly out from beneath the shower and against the concrete blocks where my balls shriveled in the cooler air removed from the hot water and steam. I crossed my arms over my chest like a shy girl in a bikini and peered through the water still pouring from the shower head and through the mist and steam rising from the floor. I felt a presence more than I could actually see anyone.

"Moose?" I said hesitantly.

There was no response, but the water running into the drain in the floor at the base of the shower pole was streaked with blood.

I lunged toward the pole, turned the shower handle to its center "Off" position, and waited for the steam to dissipate. When it did, I stood alone, naked and shivering.

"Farrell," a voice called from the lockers. "You need a ride?" Scagnetti asked. "I'm going your way."

"Um, yeah. Give me a second to towel off and gather my stuff."

"Hurry your ass. Moose's wake's in an hour. It's going to be a madhouse."

After Scags had dropped me off at my house and before leaving for the funeral home, I stole the entire pill bottle of Vicodin from the medicine cabinet while my mom and dad were engrossed by the Ohio Lottery drawing on the television. They were both lottery addicts. Bo barked his disapproval, but I gave him a harmless kick, threw a pill down, and chased it with a swig of milk directly from a gallon jug in the refrigerator.

Chapter Eight

Tuesday Evening, October 30, 201_

The Zucker and Son Funeral Home was the only one in Goodness Falls. It was once a large, two-story home on Main Street on the eastern edge of downtown. Main Street continued until it dead ended into Washington Street just over a hundred yards or so north of where Mr. Mooseburger's semi smashed into the Thompsons' oak. Long before I was born, Mr. Zucker had purchased and reconfigured the building with a crematorium and embalming station in the basement, a private living space on the second floor, and twin parlors side-by-side on the first. The eponymous Mr. Zucker had died years ago, but he still resided in his place of work inside an urn on a mantle in the long hallway/lobby that separated the two parlors. The Son was the only surviving Zucker.

When I drove past the funeral home, the receiving line stretched down the front porch, along the Main Street sidewalk, over the road bridge that crossed the creek just beyond the falls, and wrapped around the corner north on Washington Street. Football players from every school in our conference dotted the line inside their letter jackets or football jerseys. There seemed to be more people in line than actually lived in Goodness Falls. There were guys we had played ball with who had graduated and had come back from college to pay their respects. There was even a television crew from a Toledo news station shooting a remote. Kids who made merciless fun of Moose when he was the fat kid in elementary school were huddled in small groups, hugging one another and crying on each others' shoulders as if they had been best of friends with him.

"This is bullshit," I said to myself and parked the Ranger in the bank parking lot up the street.

I walked along the line – ignoring the belated congratulations and anticipatory good lucks from those waiting – and searched for Caly, who, because she was grounded from driving, I knew would be with her parents.

"T.J.!" A vaguely familiar voice rose above the din of the crowd.

Among the darkly-clad mourners, I saw the raised hand and purple nails of Mr. Mortis and stepped towards his position in the line. He waited in front of a punky girl with night-black hair in a pixie haircut beneath a black skull cap. I recognized her as the girl who had kissed Moose on the field after Friday's victory and assumed that she must have only recently transferred into Goodness Falls High School. A lot of the kids of Mexican migrant laborers transferred in and out of the school, but that was usually during the planting and harvesting seasons. The latter had just ended. She couldn't have really known Moose, and it kind of pissed me off that she was at his wake like all the others just creeping on the grief. I flashed her a dirty look, but her gaze was locked in on her black, lace-up combat boots.

"You're here," I stupidly stated the obvious when I drew near to Mr. Mortis. "I thought you had an appointment or something in Toledo."

"I took care of it already. I had to be here too. Chief Johnson likes to tell me I'm ubiquitous." He leaned towards me as if sharing a secret, "It means everywhere at the same time. The Chief learned it off of his . . ."

"Word-a-Day calendar."

"Yes. You know about that."

"He told me. I'm surprised that you know the Chief so well."

"He and I cross paths more than you might imagine."

I didn't respond, in fact, I changed the subject, but I couldn't help but wonder what Chief Johnson and a substitute teacher and rumored death metal guitarist could have in common. My thoughts turned to Moose, both the corporeal Moose lying in his casket and the ethereal Moose, who kept appearing to me. "Do you believe in ghosts, Mr. Mortis?" In that moment, he seemed the right person to ask.

"There are more things in heaven and earth, Horatio, than are dreamt of in your philosophy.'"

"Shakespeare?"

"*Hamlet.*"

"What's it mean?"

"It means that the human mind is incapable of grasping all that it wishes to know."

"Then you do believe in ghosts?"

"I didn't say that. No," he answered definitively. "There are no such things as ghosts. I wish there were, but there is only alive or dead. No in-between. No next world. Why do you ask?"

"Don't think I'm crazy, but I keep seeing Moose. I've even talked to him, and he's talked back."

"Is that what happened today in class?"

"Yeah."

"You're not crazy, T.J. People see what they want to see, or to be more accurate, what they *need* to see. It doesn't make it real nor them crazy."

I thought about his answer for a few moments. "It's good to see you here, Mr. Mortis."

"Is it? In my job, I'm not used to such welcoming sentiment from teenagers."

"You mean as a substitute teacher?"

"That too."

"I'll see you in class tomorrow," I said and began to walk away.

"Maybe you will; maybe you won't."

"What do you mean?"

"It's difficult to say where I'll be from one day to the next."

I didn't understand, but I nodded in confused agreement. "Take it easy, Mr. Mortis."

"I always do," he said. "T.J." he called once more and stopped me as I walked away. "The truth will out.'"

I understood each word but the phrasing threw me. "What?" I asked.

"The truth will out," he said. "It's from *The Merchant of Venice*. Shakespeare."

"Oh," I said, continued on, and dismissed it as another of Mr. Mortis's growing list of eccentricities.

I spotted the Stones near the front steps to the funeral home.

"Hey," I said when Caly noticed my approach. She stepped immediately out of line and met me removed from her still-stewing parents.

"What happened at practice?" Caly demanded sans a hello. "It's all over the Twitterhood that you got benched. Even my father heard about it. He's not happy. He pulled a lot of strings to get the Toledo coach down here for Friday night."

"Friday's a long way off. I'm not worried."

"But what if you don't play? What will happen to the scholarship?"

"I don't know. They have me on tape. Maybe that'll be enough. What about your parents? They still look pretty pissed," I said, peering over her shoulder.

"They'll get over it. Give them time. Everyone's upset over the accident."

"What about us?"

Caly took my hands into hers and looked up into my eyes. "We're going to get through this. We're good." Rising to her tiptoes, she kissed me and whispered, "Always . . ."

". . . and forever," I said and kissed her again with one eye on the divided Stones. The Mrs. turned her head in disgust while Dr. Stone seemed relieved to see Caly and I patching up our relationship. His daughter was his deepest hook for reeling me into and keeping me inside his un-holey boat of lies.

I joined Caly and her parents in line. As we stepped into the light and warmth of the funeral home lobby, Coach Harris, looking madly uncomfortable inside his suit, squeezed past us on his way out.

"Don't even say it," Caly warned before I could open my mouth and express my consternation.

*****

We signed our names to the guest register just outside the decorative French doors that opened into the parlor. Caly took my hand. We both took deep breaths, and when the line surged forward, we stepped inside. She began to cry and I knew she had taken a peek at the casket. I put my arm around her shoulder and hugged her close, but I couldn't lift my eyes from the floor.

It wasn't until we stood next in line and waited for Mrs. Mooseburger and a woman I assumed to be her sister to finish accepting the condolences of the Stones that I raised my eyes towards where Moose lay inside a massive but closed coffin. A montage of photographs, his home jersey inside a glass frame, his camo gear and hunting rifles decorously-arranged, and bouquet after bouquet of flowers surrounded the coffin. I pictured Moose's face as it had appeared to me in English class and understood why the coffin was closed. Perhaps it was the surreal nature of the scene or maybe it was the shocking realization that it should have been me lying there sucked dry inside that coffin, but I didn't cry. I just stared.

"T.J." Caly called to me in my transfixed state. "T.J." She repeated through her continued simpering.

"What?"

Caly nodded in the direction of Mrs. Mooseburger, who stood waiting to receive us. She went ahead while I introduced myself to Moose's aunt. Caly hugged his mother. I heard her say, "I'm so sorry for your loss."

"It's okay, dear," she said in a hoarse and fast-fading voice.

Contrary to her voice, Mrs. Mooseburger was in firm control of her emotions. If she had cried, she had done so in private. Ironically, she provided more comfort to those paying her condolences than vice versa. When it was my turn, she wrapped her thick arms around me and pressed her cheek against my chest. We separated and she signaled with her finger for me to lean over. I did so and turned my ear toward her.

"He's gone," she whispered. "around four o'clock this afternoon. The doctors were right after all. My husband passed away."

A sudden surge in the receiving line pushed us along and away from Moose's mom and up against his coffin. We bowed our heads. While Caly knelt and prayed, it struck me that Mr. Mortis's appointment in Toledo had been at four o'clock. I'm not even sure why I made the connection, but it sent an ice cold shiver up my spine.

Chapter Nine

Wednesday Morning, Halloween, October 31, 201_

I had a shitty night's sleep. The single Vicodin I took failed to adequately dull the pain in my head nor did it induce the needed degree of drowsiness. The coincidence of Mr. Mortis's arrival in Goodness Falls and the deaths of Mrs. Miller, Moose, and his dad and my own near-collision with their semi seemed auspicious. It tortured my thoughts. But why? What could be the connection if any?

Sometime around three in the morning, I slipped a highlight disc of my and Moose's junior football season into a portable DVD player. I watched with it resting on my chest. Footage from every game was spliced together with scenes from pep rallies, team feeds, homecoming festivities, and candid sideline shots. Cheesy songs, chosen by some parent with a penchant for rock ballads from the eighties, played throughout the disc.

I paused the disc on a shot of Moose and me with our sweaty cheeks covered with smeared eye black. We sat side-by-side on the bench just after we'd been pulled from the game. Each of us had one arm wrapped around the other's shoulders, and both of our other arms were upraised and signaling #1. I stared at that frame of film until I stumbled into a fitful asleep. When I woke at seven a.m. to the sound of my phone alarm, a screensaver on the DVD player had replaced our smiling faces. Determined not to allow the throbbing in my skull to win, I gritted my teeth and prepared for what would be one of the most strange and eventful days of my life.

*****

I didn't own a suit, so my mom had laid out my dad's from their wedding. He was more-than-happy to allow me to wear it; it gave him an excuse not to go. The suit was at least a decade-and-a-half out of style: a double breasted, three-button jacket with matching pleated pants that bulged embarrassingly in the front. The jacket was too tight through the shoulders and the pants through the butt and thighs. Although my dad and I were of almost the exact same height, all of the weightlifting I'd done for football had added a good fifteen pounds of muscle to my frame. All-in-all, the suit looked nothing like the streamlined, modern-cut ones that Dr. Stone wore.

Any student with a note from his or her parents was excused from morning classes to attend the funeral at Faith Lutheran Church, which was on the opposite side of the street from the funeral home and within easy walking distance of the school. The fact that Caly and I each had to go with our own families was fine with me because Mrs. Mooseburger had requested six senior football players to serve as pall bearers: five of Moose's offensive linemen buddies and me. Therefore, I wouldn't be able to sit with Caly anyway, nor would I be forced to sit with my mom, who had no idea of how close she'd come to being the grieving mother on that morning.

The six of us pallbearers gathered early inside the vestibule of the church in order to receive our instructions from Mr. Zucker. As we waited for the hearse, mourners began to arrive. We formed two lines of three facing each other and acted as unofficial greeters. The pews filled quickly. The Stones arrived in their freshly detailed Escalade. I wondered how long before the body work would be completed on the Benz. I also wondered who was the other woman, smothered in whose perfume Dr. Stone returned to the football game at Toledo, and for whom he had most likely purchased the Cabriolet and from whom he had borrowed it.

Caly gave my hand a reassuring squeeze as she passed. Her parents nodded but said nothing.

Cory Morrison gave all of the guys high fives as he passed through except for me.

Coach Harris entered in front of his pack of assistant coaches and pretty much ignored all of us pallbearers.

Chief Johnson arrived in full dress uniform. When he shook my hand, waves of guilt coursed through me.

"You okay, T.J?" He asked and lingered.

"Yes, sir."

"This is going to be a rough day for everyone. Just think of poor Mrs. Mooseburger," he said. "But, hey, did you hear about the Mr.?"

I played dumb and shook my head.

"He passed away yesterday."

"He did?"

"I was there when he died."

"You were?"

"And you know what?"

"What's that?"

"Just before he died, he woke up."

"Did he say anything about the accident?" I asked a little too prematurely and with too keen of an interest.

The Chief cocked his head to the side and looked deeply into my eyes. "I can't tell you that."

I tried to cover my curiosity. "That's great," I said.

"Great?" The Chief questioned my enthusiasm.

"I mean that Mr. Mooseburger woke up, not that he died." I desperately tried not to wear my concern all over my face.

"We've all been under a lot of stress, but it looks like 'The truth will out' after all."

"What? Wait. What's that?"

"Oh, I'm sorry. It's just something Angel Mortis said to me the other day. It's from Shakespeare. *The Merchant of Venice,* I believe he said."

"Angel?" I asked.

"Yes. You know him. He's subbing up at the high school."

"I know *Mr.* Mortis. I didn't know his name is Angel though."

"I think it's Hispanic or Latin-something. Hey! Speak of the devil. There he is."

I looked out through the church doors and down the steps to where Mr. Mortis stood in the parking space reserved for the hearse. He was checking his watch repeatedly.

"Okay then, T.J. I'm sure we'll talk again," the Chief said and entered the church.

I thought, "The truth will out?!' We'll talk again?!" What did he mean? What did he know?" I felt the nausea rising and began to sweat profusely and suspiciously in my ill-fitting suit. I hurried to the men's room, where I fortuitously found Dr. Stone straightening his tie and studying his face in a full-length mirror against the wall.

"He knows," I said while splashing water on my face and hands and surreptitiously removing and swallowing another Vicodin from the fast-emptying bottle.

"Who knows what?" Dr. Stone asked.

"The Chief. I think he knows something."

"Why do you say that?" He asked while running a comb through his hair.

"Mr. Mooseburger. Before he died, he came out of his coma."

"That's impossible. I checked his charts myself this morning."

"I'm just telling you what the Chief told me."

"The Chief's just fishing. That's all. Even if Mooseburger did come out of it, I told you that he most likely won't have remembered a thing about the accident. Besides, he would have still been under heavy sedation; nothing he would have said could be admissible in court." Dr. Stone continued to style his thick blond hair as if we were discussing the weather rather than the possible ruination of our futures.

"You also said he wouldn't wake up."

"Okay," he grew impatient. "Say he did remember and he shared his version of the accident with the Chief. What proof is there?"

"What about the Benz?"

"I've already told you. I took the Benz to a mechanic friend for a tune-up, but just to cover our bases, if anyone asks – which they won't – we say we drove the Cabriolet to and from Toledo."

"Whose is it?" I asked.

"Whose is what?"

"The Cabriolet."

"Look, T.J. You're almost a grown man. I'm going to share something with you." He stopped his primping, turned to face me, and looked me straight in the eyes. "It's something I need for you to keep just between us men – something to show you the trust I have in you and you should have in me."

"You don't have to . . ."

"I want to. I have a colleague at the hospital, a nurse. She's just a very good friend, but you know my wife. Anyway, you were right. The Cabriolet is not a loaner; it belongs to her. She's letting me borrow it for a few days until the Benz is out of the shop. It's saving me the trouble and expense of renting a car, not to mention the suspicion that might arouse."

"What about the Chief?"

"There's nothing to worry about as long as we stay a team and stick to our story."

I must have been stupidly moved by the trust Dr. Stone exhibited in me, or maybe I was flattered by his buddying up. I'm not sure which, but I found myself in a confessional mood. "I'm not sure I even care about getting caught. It's the lies and the guilt that are messing with my head. This is going to sound crazy, but I've seen Moose three times since the accident."

"You what?"

"Moose. I've seen him. I've talked to him. And I think Mr. Mortis . . ."

"What? Who is Mr. Mortis?"

"He's a substitute teacher."

"What could he have to do with anything?"

"I'm not sure, but he arrived the morning after Mrs. Miller's death. I saw him the morning of the accident, and he was in Toledo at exactly the same time that Mr. Mooseburger died."

Mr. Stone looked at me as if I had completely lost my mind. "T.J. Look. I don't know a thing about this Mr. Mortis, but as for Moose, that's just grief. It's not unusual to hallucinate or dream . . ."

"These weren't hallucinations or dreams. I was wide awake each time."

"Okay. Whatever. I know some very good counselors at the hospital. When things settle down, I'll hook you up with one, and you can work your way through all of this, but right now and for the rest of today, you've got to get your head together. You may not care 'about getting caught,' but you weren't driving. It's my ass that would be in a sling, and don't forget that I was only there in the first place because I was trying to help you out. To get you that scholarship."

"I know. I know it would only mean more suffering for more people, but still it's making me crazy."

Dr. Stone washed and dried his hands. "Keep your shit together, son. And remember, what I told you about my friend and the car is between us guys."

"Yes sir," I said.

Dr. Stone exited the men's room.

The unexpected flush of a toilet in one of the two stalls surprised the shit right out of me. I slowly crouched in order to peek beneath the stall door, where I saw a pair of blue jeans puddled over a pair of work boots, covered in dried dirt.

I stood back up. "Moose?" I asked through the metal door, but I received no response. "Moose?" I repeated more loudly, but once again, there was no answer.

The silver latch on the stall door began to turn. It clicked open. I could see the steel toes of the boots pointing towards me from under the door. The stall door swung open a few inches.

"Moose?" I asked one more time.

"Ahhhhhh!" A guy I'd never seen before in my life screamed when he exited the bathroom stall to see me standing staring at him like an idiot. "Dude!" He said and bent over to catch his stolen breath. He wore a pair of expensive, over-the-ear, noise cancellation headphones, which he removed and draped around his neck. The tinny sound of heavy metal guitars poured from the headphones. Seeing my suit, he must have thought I was somebody important or at least somebody who would take offense for his using the church bathroom. "Dude," he repeated, "I'm sorry but I had to take a dump. It was an emergency."

I stared stupidly as he continued his unnecessary apology.

"All we got at the cemetery is a port-o-potty, and it ain't been emptied in weeks. I had a break while waiting for this funeral to get over and thought I could sneak in. I'm really sorry, dude."

I needed air. Without a word, I turned, exited the restroom, and instead of returning to the church vestibule, I walked out a side door into a small garden courtyard with an artificial pond in the center, several park benches along a circular walkway, and a single Japanese maple with its purplish leaves stubbornly resisting Autumn's demand for tribute. I surprised a girl who dropped her cigarette and ducked behind the tree.

"I saw you," I said, but she didn't respond.

She slowly tilted her head out from behind the trunk until it was cocked at a forty-five degree angle. It was the girl from the line outside the funeral home.

"I saw you in line last night," I said in an accusatory tone. "How did you know Moose?"

She sidestepped out from behind the tree. "Who's Moose?"

"David Mooseburger. Moose. The funeral. I saw you kiss him after the game last Friday."

"You did? I did? I don't know. I was pretty fucked up."

"Then why were you at the wake last night?"

"I just saw the line and got in it. I thought it might be a club or something cool. Then this morning, I overheard some chicks in the girls' room talking about the funeral. They said if you had a note you could get out of morning classes, so I wrote one and forged my uncle's signature. Besides, I kind of like funerals."

I ignored the bizarre "I kind of like funerals" comment. "Why your 'uncle's' signature?"

"Because my crack-whoring bitch of a mom died and left me alone, so I had to move to this shithole with my uncle. He's been an angel."

"But you're wearing all-black like you planned on coming."

"I always wear black." She said it like, "Duh!"

I didn't even know her name, nor had I noticed her at school or her fashion choices: black combat boots over black thigh highs, a short black skirt that pushed the upper limits of the school's dress code, the same black-knit skull cap, and a black hoodie, over a black tank. All of which matched her short black hair with royal blue streaks and her heavy black eye liner. She looked a little like Kate Beckinsale in those vampires versus the werewolves movies or what I imagined Mr. Mortis would look like if he were a teenage girl.

"I've got to get back," I said.

"Whatever," she said. But after I'd turned away and was reaching for the door handle, she said, "Was he a friend of yours? This Moose guy."

"My best friend."

She held out her pack of cigarettes toward me. "You want one?"

"No. I don't smoke."

She stuffed the pack inside her combat boot. "I'm sorry about your friend, T.J."

"I'm sorry too, . . ." I waited for her to fill in the blank.

"Perdita."

*****

By the time I returned to the rear of the church, the hearse had arrived and parked on the street outside. Mrs. Mooseburger stood with her sister next to the hearse and waited for her boy to be removed. I hurried to join the other pallbearers at the back of the hearse and passed Mr. Mortis on my way. He wore a smile incongruous to the occasion.

"T.J.," he greeted me and held out his hand to shake. His hands were remarkably cold for a moderate day in October. "Well, we were born to die.'"

"Don't tell me. Shakespeare?"

"*Romeo and Juliet.*"

"Don't you have class?" I asked.

"Conference period. Thought I'd pay my respects. See you inside," he said and continued on into the church.

I was surprised by how light the coffin was as we lifted it from the back of the hearse and carried it up the church steps to a waiting casket cart. The minister met the casket and greeted Mrs. Mooseburger and her sister with condolences. He said a brief prayer then lead our somber procession into the church.

A tsunami of pain washed through my head the moment we entered the church. It may have been the sudden transition from light to dark. I don't know, but the pain almost dropped me to my knees. The fucking Vicodin I'd taken in the men's room hadn't kicked in. I squinted and scanned the pews as we entered the crowded nave. The rear ones were filled with students: some who were sincerely in mourning and many who were simply taking advantage of a morning excused from classes. In the front, one side was reserved for the football team and cheerleaders and the other side for friends and family of the Mooseburgers. As we wheeled Moose up the aisle and into position in front of the raised altar, I was surprised and pissed off to see Caly seated next to Pete Terwilliger. At several points during the service, I caught her leaning her head against Terwilliger's shoulder and him giving her one-armed, consolatory hugs. I'd never been particularly jealous; Caly had never given me reason to be. But something about their canoodling got inside my head and wormed its poisonous way into my brain.

By Mrs. Mooseburger's request, the final interment at the cemetery was restricted to family. So after returning Moose's coffin to the hearse, I waited for Caly outside the front of church.

"What the hell was all that about?" I ambushed her after she had kissed her parents goodbye with a violent grab of her elbow.

"What was what about?"

"You and Terwilliger! You may as well have been fucking him?" Even as I said the words, I realized how stupid, obscene, and unfair they were.

"What!?"

I already regretted my accusation, but I was unable to unsay it or to stop myself from pressing forward. "You heard me."

"Who are you?" Caly scrunched up her face and asked.

"Caly," I tried to soften my tone. "I'm . . ."

"Don't! Don't even say you're sorry." She took a deep breath and impressively regained her composure. "I'm going to school. I can't miss physics."

"Let me walk you."

"No!" She threw her arms down at her side and turned her head away. "I don't want to talk to you right now. I don't even want to see you." She spun on her heels and stormed away.

"Smooth." An unfamiliar voice commented from behind me. "Your girlfriend?"

I looked over my shoulder. She hadn't been there a moment ago, at least I hadn't seen her if she was, but it was Perdita. "Maybe," I said, no longer sure myself.

"You wanna ditch?"

"Ditch?"

"Yeah. Skip class."

"And do what?"

"I don't know. Seize the day. Have some fun. How about we take a ride into Sandusky? Hang out there."

"I don't have a car."

Perdita opened her hand. Dangling from her middle finger was a key ring. "They're Mr. Mortis's. I stole them from his pocket when he was giving me a hug. He won't miss them or the car until after school. We can be back by then. He'll think he left them in the ignition."

I considered going back to school, listening to Mr. Mortis drone on about *Macbeth* or *Hamlet* or some dark shit like that, and of being ignored by Caly for the rest of the day. "Why not?" I said. "As long as I'm back in time for practice. But you're going to have to drive."

"Why's that?" Perdita asked.

I removed the pill bottle from my suit coat pocket and held it up for her to see. "I've been taking these."

"Nice," she said.

"You know what they are?" I asked.

"Vicodin. I take them for menstrual migraines and . . ."

"'And' what?"

"For fun."

Considering how she had stolen the keys, I stuffed the bottle deep into my pants pocket.

Chapter Ten

Wednesday Afternoon, Halloween, October 31, 201_

We drove the fewer than ten miles into Sandusky and headed for the downtown, where we parked on Columbus Avenue outside of the Erie County Courthouse and beneath its four-sided, moon-faced clock tower.

"What now?" I asked once we'd exited the wagon and began walking aimlessly north towards the Sandusky Bay.

"First, we need to get you out of those clothes," Perdita said.

"Sounds like fun."

"Not like that, stupid. We need to get you into something a little less conspicuous."

"And exactly how are we going to do that?" I asked.

"You got any money?"

"A little."

"It won't take much."

"What won't?"

She pointed ahead.

Where the land began its slow descent towards the shoreline, a red Salvation Army Thrift Store sign hung over the sidewalk.

"Let's go pop some tags," I said.

Perdita laughed and we took off in a jog.

The grossly obese woman, who sat at the checkout counter intently focused on her word search puzzle, didn't so much as raise her eyes when we walked in. A few equally-disinterested employees stood sorting recently-arrived donations on top of long, rectangular tables in the middle of the store.

A mother, with three dirty-faced, pre-school aged children in tow, roamed the aisles.

Perdita led me to the men's section of gently-used clothing. "What's your pants size?" She asked.

"I don't know. 32 X 34 or something like that."

She moved to the appropriate circular rack, "Put out your arms," she ordered. I complied and Perdita began to pile pants choices across them.

"What about tops?"

"Tops?"

"Shirts. What's your shirt size?"

"I don't know. My mom buys all my clothes."

"She probably lays them out for you too."

"What?"

Perdita laughed. "Nothing. Let's go with large."

In what appeared to be completely random selection, she added one shirt after another over my outstretched arms.

"What do you want to be for Halloween?" She asked. "Preppy?"

"What?"

"It's Halloween."

"It is?"

"It's my favorite holiday. So what do you want to be? A hippie?"

"No."

"A Hipster?"

"No."

"Gangsta?" She formed an X across her chest and fashioned some kind of gang signs with her fingers.

"No!"

"Glam?"

"No. I don't even know what that is."

"Well, you got to be something."

"Give me a minute," I said. I threw all of her selections for me on top of a rack of coats and began to rummage through the clothes islands of misfits and castaways until I came away satisfied and carrying a pair of boot-cut jeans, a Navajo plaid western shirt with two breast pockets and pearl snaps for buttons, a pair of cowboy boots, and a Stetson.

"A hick? You want to be a hick."

"I *am* a hick. What I *want* to be is a cowboy."

"Seems like the same thing to me, but it's your disguise, gaucho."

There were so few customers in the store, Perdita was able to sneak me into the ladies' changing area, which consisted of a long hallway in the rear of the store with a series of cubicles cordoned off by rollaway walls with shower curtains for doors.

When I was shirtless and changing into the jeans, Perdita stuck her head through the curtain just as I was pulling them over my boxers.

"Hey!" I said embarrassed and nearly bare assed. "That's not fair."

"La vida no esta justa," she called and retreated into the narrow hallway. "Life's not fair. Get over it."

"You sound like my football coach. That's something he'd say," I said, as I pulled back the curtain and walked out into the hallway

"Turn around," she said. "Let me get a good look."

I did as she ordered.

"You know, you *are* one fine looking cowboy, but you totally suck at going incognito. The idea when ditching school is to be inconspicuous. Sandusky, Ohio, ain't Dodge City. Lose the hat, shirt, and sunglasses. Keep the jeans – for me."

"Okay. But what about you. What would you like to be?"

"Alive," I'm pretty sure she said. But before I could question her, a dreamy expression transformed Perdita's face. She disappeared inside the store for a few minutes. When she returned, she stepped behind the dressing room curtain then reemerged wearing a sleeveless, soft white and pink floral cotton sundress with a scoop neck and short skirt; it was totally out-of-season but totally gorgeous. She wore white high heels; a string of imitation pearls draped around her neck; and a wide-brimmed, pink, straw sun hat. "What do you think?" She asked.

"Wow" was all I could think to say.

"That's what I hoped you'd say."

I drank her in from top to bottom. "You're . . . you're beautiful."

"Really?"

"Drop dead gorgeous," I said.

Her expression turned gloomy. "Thanks, but don't get used to the fancy dress."

"Why?"

"I can't wear this out there. We're supposed to blend in. I don't think this," Perdita ran her hands over the dress from her breasts, down her sides, and past her hips, "would help with that."

"I guess you're right," I said, "but can I look one more time?"

She performed a quick step away from me and an exaggerated catwalk twirl, then she literally leaped into my arms, draped hers around my neck, and wrapped her legs tightly around my hips, which caused the dress to ride high over her bare thighs. Perdita looked deeply into my eyes with her lips no more than a few inches from mine before sliding down me to the floor as if I were a fireman's pole.

"I suppose that's the pill bottle in your pocket," she teased when her feet touched tile.

"No," I answered. "I left it in the suit pants."

"T.J. Farrell!" She said in mock disgust and delivered a playful, two-handed shove to my chest before retreating once more into the dressing room.

I put on the clothes she had chosen for me: a pair of black canvas sneakers, the jeans, and a chocolate brown sweatshirt with the hood up and covering my head. I think she was going for skater. When she returned, she was back in her everyday black.

I removed the pill bottle from the pants pocket and dropped my father's suit into a donation box on our way out the door and into a downtown Sandusky noon hour.

We bought two gyros and a coke from a food cart vendor outside the courthouse, where we sat on a bench in the park in the sun and ate our lunches. After we'd finished, we walked down to the Jackson Street Pier on the Sandusky Bay and sat on the end with our legs draped over the side. We watched as a freighter inched its way through the shipping channel towards the coal docks on the west end of town. For ninety minutes, we talked about everything; we talked about nothing. I actually don't remember one thing we discussed, but I know it wasn't high school or college or any of the Stone family or football or Moose or anything remotely Goodness Falls-related.

When the courthouse clock chimed to indicate two-thirty, I got up to go. I must have stood up too quickly, for my head began to spin wildly. I dropped to my knees to avoid stumbling into the water and drowning.

"Are you okay?" Perdita asked.

"My headache's back," I said, leaned back, and removed the pill bottle from my jeans pocket. With my hands shaking, I struggled to unscrew the childproof lid, poured a pill into my left palm, and was about to throw it back when Perdita stopped my hand.

"It sucks that's all you've got. Vikes are okay; Percs or Oxies are the shit. But here," she said. "Give it to me. I can make it better."

I hesitated.

"C'mon. Give it to me."

I was afraid that I might not get it back, but I did as she asked.

She took from her pocket the foil gyro wrapper then searched for a stone in between the concrete walkway and the steel facing of the pier. When she found one of adequate size, she placed the Vicodin tablet inside the foil on the concrete and pressed and crushed it with the stone.

"Hey!" I protested.

"Give me two more. Trust me," she said. I hesitated but every second I waited was another second of unalleviated and excruciating agony. Perdita peeled my fingers open one at a time and removed the bottle from my hand. She poured out two more pills and pulverized and mixed them in with the first. She folded the foil in half to gather the Vicodin dust then poured it onto the palm of her hand. "Hillbilly heroin," she said. "It works faster and better when you snort it."

She raised her open hand towards my face. I bent over to meet her halfway, pressed one nostril against my nose with my fingers, and snorted the dust through my other. At first, it felt as if I'd inhaled hundreds of tiny shards of glass and it burned like hell, but it soon did as she promised and worked at least twice as fast and felt twice as euphoric. I lifted my face to Perdita and smiled.

"Let's go," she said. "We need to get the car back."

Chapter Eleven

Wednesday Afternoon, Halloween, October 31, 201_

Wednesday was the last day of practice in full pads. With everyone still in a funereal mood, the senior section of the locker room lacked its typical pre-practice horseplay, but with the Vicodin flooding my system, my head felt as good as it had since I took the initial hit the previous Friday. I felt like a freaking super-hero. During the quarterbacks' film session and the offensive game plan meeting, Coach McKuen didn't quiz me once regarding my reads: a bad sign as to the coaches' intention of playing me on Friday, but it was also a good thing because I had been unable to memorize them anyway, and I was too hyped in that condition to answer any questions.

The good news was that I was spared Goon Squad duty, and for the first two-thirds of practice, everything ran smoothly. I bore my demoted status stoically, firmly believing Coach Harris was bluffing and it was only a matter of time before I'd be reinstated as the starter. He had to know I was his best chance for earning that two hundredth victory.

Both the offense and defense seemed to click during individual position and group periods. That changed, however, during the fifteen minute, full-go ones vs. ones session at the end of practice. Terwilliger's mechanics and play execution, which had been so smooth during drills and against the Goonies, suddenly abandoned him in the face of varsity speed and tenacity. His passes were off-target and mistimed. He threw repeatedly into coverage and failed to make the appropriate reads and audibles. Flustered, at one point he fumbled two consecutive snaps from Scags and angrily spiked the ball into the ground in frustration.

Behind my face mask, I did my best to keep my composure solid and my smile hidden. I humbly carried out my duties as the back-up quarterback and charted the plays as they were called. After several particularly poor decisions by Terwilliger, I saw Coach McKuen look pleadingly to Coach Harris for a change in quarterbacks. Instead, Harris called a series of running plays requiring nothing more difficult than a hand-off from Terwilliger.

In preparation for the possibility of a game night injury to the starter, the number two quarterback was typically given the last few snaps of Wednesday practices. Harris eyeballed the third-string quarterback, Lance Green, but he was a sophomore whose hairless balls would have retreated into his belly quicker than a turtle inside his shell should he be called on to take varsity snaps. Coach Harris had no choice but to insert me to run the final five plays with the number one offense.

On the first play, Morrison purposefully whiffed on his block of the backside defensive end, who blindsided me and forced a fumble. Coach Harris tore into me for not progressing through my reads quickly enough. "For Christ's sake, Farrell, you can't expect your blockers to hold them all day! Get rid of the damn ball!"

In the huddle, Morrison smirked in self-satisfaction, "Maybe you should go back to the Goonies, asshole," he said.

Morrison received neither laughter nor derision from the rest of the huddle.

"Just do your job, Morrison. And I'll do mine. All right?"

Coach called for a sprint out pass into a trips formation, which meant, if I was fast enough, I could outrun the play side defensive end regardless of the "lookout block" – the kind where the blocker misses his man then turns around and yells, "Look out!" – which I anticipated from Morrison.

On "Hut," with sheer speed, I was able to gain the edge and avoid the sack. The trips receivers executed a flood route into zone coverage, which effectively layered them and forced two defensive backs to choose which two of the three receivers to defend. I found the open man and delivered a precise spiral for a big gain.

With similar results over the next three plays, I began to win back the support of *my* offense, excluding Morrison, who with me out of the line-up, expected to be the "go-to" guy on Friday night versus Lakeview. It was only four plays, but Coach Harris's substitution of me for the inexperienced Terwilliger had made it abundantly clear how much the offense relied on its usual trigger man. It was obvious – to everyone except Coach Harris at least – that, if we were going to make a state run, they would need me playing quarterback.

Practice ended on a high note and the locker room returned to its sophomoric antics. I was allowed back inside the circle by slow degrees, one smart ass remark at a time. They rained down upon me as I stood beneath a steaming-hot showerhead.

"So, Farrell, who'd you blow to get back in the line-up?" A voice asked.

"Did Caly's daddy threaten to fire Coach again?" Another asked.

"I heard it was Coach Markinson at Toledo who made the call," someone else answered.

I said nothing. I had let my play on the practice field earn my readmission to the pack and hopefully back into the starting lineup, but that was out of my hands. At least for a while, thanks to Perdita's hillbilly heroin, I had been able to forget about Moose, Caly, Coach Harris, Dr. Stone, Chief Johnson, and the pain.

At least for a while.

*****

Basking in what appeared to be a return to normalcy, I dilly-dallied while getting dressed and packing up my practice gear, so that by the time I'd finished, I was the only upperclassmen still in the locker room. Therefore, I was stranded without a ride. For the past two years, Moose had always taken me home after practice. If, for whatever reason, Moose wasn't available, I'd bum a ride off of someone else. If totally desperate, I'd call my mom. Not wanting a face-to-face with Coach Harris, who was still shooting-the-post-practice-shit with the other coaches in their office, I stepped outside to call home. It was a cloudless night well-lit by a three-quarters moon. But before I could even raise my "Contacts" on my cell, a pair of headlamps froze me like a spotlighted deer. The deep and rich sound of the horn on the Escalade beeped, and Caly pulled up in front of me.

The passenger side window descended. "Get in," she said. I did as ordered and threw my equipment bag on a back seat.

"Where we going?" I asked.

"You'll see," she said. "We need to talk and you need to see somebody." Caly pulled out of the lot and turned left onto BR 101 in the exact same careless manner of her father that had initiated that worst week of my life.

I bit my tongue.

She turned left once more at the four-way and drove past the front of the high school towards town. Along the way, we passed a number of costumed trick-or-treaters.

"How'd you get a car? Aren't you grounded?"

"I haven't been home yet from school and cheer practice. Those are my two exceptions. Remember?"

"Right. Hey, I'm really sorry about today," I said as we crossed the bridge and passed the falls. "I've been getting these headaches, and they're making me see and say crazy things."

"Still?"

"Still," I said.

"Have you told Schultzie or gone to a doctor?"

"I can't. If I do, my season is over. I can't have another concussion on my medical record. Shit, if Toledo finds out about my concussions, they'll never offer me that full ride."

"So what if they don't, Teege? We'll figure something else out. Daddy will . . ."

"Daddy will what? Pay my tuition?"

"I don't know what, but it's not worth risking your health for."

"That's easy for you to say."

"Don't go there. It's not my fault my family has money."

I let it drop. What I really wanted to say was that her driving wasn't helping my headache, but for the sake of not hurting her feelings once again, I kept my mouth shut.

I don't want this to sound sexist, but the truth is that Caly was the worst driver I'd ever shared a ride with. I think it was the "little girl in a big vehicle" syndrome. Her father would have put her in a tank to protect her if it were street legal. Instead, he kept seating her behind the wheel of some of the biggest SUVs on the road. Her car previous to the Escalade had been a black Hummer, but she kept banging into the side of their garage, shearing off mirrors, and running over curbs and into mostly stationary objects. She took corners like a formula-one driver, ran drag races between stop signs, slammed on the brakes, and had the most annoying tendency of jerking the steering wheel left and right even when on a straightaway.

By the time she pulled into the cemetery behind Faith Lutheran Church, I was suffering from a serious case of motion sickness that inflamed the neurotransmitters in my brain and hastened the return of the dizziness and nausea. Or it may have simply been that the Vicodin had worn off.

The narrow, winding paths inside the cemetery didn't help either. I was relieved when Caly finally came to a stop in front of a newly-laid, rectangular stretch of sod, which, even in only the light of the moon and the Escalade's headlamps, was conspicuously green amongst the browning grass of mid-fall that surrounded it.

"What are we doing here?" I asked peevishly and in no mood for the stunt Caly was pulling.

"We need to talk, T.J."

"Here! We need to talk here?" Her little psychological ploy of bringing me to Moose's grave really irritated the shit out of me, and it all but washed away any notion I'd harbored of being able to kiss and make up.

"Our problem isn't us. It's about Moose and you dealing with it – or *not* dealing with it."

"I know Moose is dead, Caly, and I know he isn't coming back. I don't need to see his fucking grave."

"See what I mean. Why do you need to curse? You never used to curse – at least not in front of me."

"I'm cursing because this is so fucking stupid."

"But you talk about Moose sometimes as if he's still alive, and you're angry whenever you're around me."

"I'm not angry at you."

"Then who? God? Moose? Yourself? My father? It was an accident, T.J. Accidents happen. That's life."

"Can't we just drop it?"

"Not now. You told my father about seeing and talking with Moose."

"Oh, Christ."

"Now, he wants you to see a psychiatrist. He's afraid of what you might do. Sweetie, I'm afraid of what you might do too.

"Oh, I get it now. He has a backup plan."

"Backup plan for what?"

"If he can get me to a psychiatrist, everyone would think I'm crazy. If I would decide to narc him out, nobody would believe me."

"Narc who out? For what? What are you talking about?" Once again, her tears began to flow generously. She leaned across the center console and reached for my hand, but I pulled it away.

My patience was exhausted. I couldn't feel sympathy nor think through my resurrected headache any longer. I reached into my jeans pocket for the Vicodin. I didn't even care about having to explain it to Caly; although, I knew she'd scold me for taking them. In the end it didn't matter; the pill bottle wasn't there. I patted my other thigh feeling for the bottle, but there was nothing. "Damn it!" I yelled and slammed my elbow into the door panel.

"T.J.!" What's wrong? What are you looking for?"

"It's none of your business!" I snapped callously and sent Caly retreating against the driver's side door and window from where she watched my frantic self pat down, my dive into the back seat, and my crazed rummaging through my equipment bag. When my search proved fruitless, I plopped back into my seat and fuzzily replayed the afternoon's events and the last time I remembered having the pill bottle in my possession. "That bitch!" I screamed and punched the leather-covered dashboard. The knuckles on my index and middle fingers split wide open and spilled blood onto the seat. I threw my hands up to the sides of my head, a movement that splattered the passenger side window with a rainbow arc of blood droplets, which beaded and ran down the glass. "She stole 'em!" I said out loud to myself. In my periphery, I saw Caly cowering with her hands drawn up in front of her in a protective manner. "Not you," I said. "I don't mean you."

"Then who do you mean? Who's a 'bitch?'" She damn near choked on the word.

"That new girl. She stole my stuff."

"What 'new girl?' What 'stuff?'"

"Perdita,"(I realized I didn't know her last name.) "something or other. She's a migrant kid, I think, just transferred in."

"I don't know who you're talking about."

"Of course, you don't. She wouldn't be in any of your fucking honors classes."

"You don't have to yell, and you don't have to swear."

"She took my headache medicine," I explained as if it would justify my rage and earn Caly's pardon.

Caly sat back up in her seat. "So you have medicine? I thought you said you hadn't seen a doctor," she said suspiciously.

"I haven't. It was my mom's. She gave it to me."

"T.J., you shouldn't . . ."

"Don't lecture me, okay! I don't need another person in my life telling me what to do or pressuring me! I just need my medicine."

With impressive temerity in the face of my enraged state, Caly ventured out onto thinning ice. "What about this girl? How do you know her?"

"She was at the funeral today."

"And . . ."

I realized I was screwed, but I couldn't stop talking. "And, we sort of played hooky this afternoon."

"Just you and her? You and this new girl named, what was it? Perdita?" Caly had regained her nerve and was on the offensive. I became the one shrinking in his seat.

"It was nothing. We just went into Sandusky, had lunch, and hung out."

"Oh, is that all? And how did you get there?"

"We took Mr. Mortis's car."

"That's just great. So, let me get this straight. You met some Mexican ho for the first time, stole a car, skipped school, and went on a date, yet you accused me of 'fucking' Pete Terwilliger because I sat next to him at a funeral?!"

Even though she was more-than-justified in her anger and I knew how pathetic I sounded, I refused to concede. Besides, my focus was being sapped by the sound, not the meanings, of each of her high-pitched words of justified condemnation. Each was a stab of an ice pick through my ear canals and into my brain. "It wasn't like that," was the best I could come up with.

"Get out," she said calmly at first. But when I didn't budge, as I was trying to process all that was happening in those tortured moments, she screamed, "GET . . . OUT!"

I did as I'd been ordered and stood with my arms at my sides in my thrift-store purchased clothes and holding my equipment bag.

Caly sped away in the Escalade. After a moment, a geyser of misdirected rage erupted inside of me. I dropped my bag and impetuously took off running after her. "Fuck you!" I yelled. "Fuck you and your murdering asshole of a father!"

I ran thirty or forty yards in futile pursuit until I dropped to my knees on the blacktop path, pressed the heels of my hands into my pulsating eyeballs, and cried and cried and cried. After I don't know how long, I walked back to where I'd dropped my bag on the grass near the path, smack dab in front of Moose's grave. "What?" I said. "Now you've got nothing to say? You don't want to show yourself? Is this some kind of fucked up revenge because I left you hanging and went on that stupid recruiting visit? Well, fuck you too, Moose. Fuck you." I actually flipped off his grave. "You know what? You're the lucky one. I'd trade places with you in a second. *Carpe Diem* my ass! This goddamned headache is making me CRAZY!" I screamed. "The Chief, Dr. Stone, Coach Harris, my mom are all up my ass, and I think I just lost my girlfriend. What's the point? I just want this headache to go AWAY!" I screamed once more.

"Hey, hey. Calm down, son. You're going to wake the dead." The voice wasn't Moose's and it came from behind me. I turned and stared into the blinding white beam of an approaching flashlight. I threw my hands over my eyes like a vampire at daybreak. The light turned off. "T.J. It's just me. Chief Johnson."

"What do you want, Chief?"

"Pastor Stephens from the church called. He said there was some ruckus going on in the cemetery. Happens every year on Halloween: kids tipping over headstones or holding séances or parking in here and making out. Which is just creepy if you ask me. Last year I ran out a whole herd of crazies playing some kind of zombie apocalypse game." He turned his flashlight back on. I followed its beam as it ran along the grass to Moose's headstone then was doused. "Moose's death has been hard on a lot of people. You ain't alone in this. And just think. In coupla more days, his daddy will be lying right beside him. It's a tragedy, really."

TY ROTH

The Chief took a protracted pause and stared through the darkness in the direction of the Mooseburger family plot before adding, "Why don't I run you home. My cruiser's back there in the lot."

I didn't say anything then or during the walk through the cemetery to the Chief's cruiser. I climbed in through the passenger side door, sat, stared out the window, and tried to isolate each throb inside my skull. I figured if I could concentrate on surviving one pulse at a time, I might be able to string enough of them together to get home without reaching for the revolver in the Chief's holster and blowing my brains out all over the inside of the cruiser.

We had only pulled out of the church parking lot when the Chief said, "I know you're probably in a hurry to get home with it being a school night and all. But, if you don't mind, I'm going to swing by Jim's Salvage yard. I want to show you something that's been bothering me."

What choice did I have?

"Sure," I answered and concentrated on surviving the next pulse.

*****

Jim's was a few minutes east of town in the opposite direction of Crystal Ridge. It crossed my mind that the Chief was fully aware of my condition, and this was his way of torturing information from me. My suspicion was heightened when he pulled up to the chained gates of the junkyard, located a Master Lock key on a massive key ring, and before getting out of the cruiser said, "This is where we impound vehicles. The Mooseburgers' semi is in the back there."

The Chief climbed out, unlocked the gates, and swung them wide open. He returned to the cruiser and slowly drove us on a circuitous course through rows of mostly junk cars and stacks of tires. The path was unpaved and each bump sent a bolt of lightning across the hemispheres of my brain. Finally, the headlights shined on the front of the Mooseburgers' semi, and I was staring once more at the license plate. It read TF 1207 not TJ 1027, which I'd misinterpreted as my missed date with . . . "

"Angel Mortis," the Chief said, seemingly apropos to nothing.

"What?"

"Angel Mortis. He's in some kind of hard rock metal band. He buys a lot of this junk *metal* – get it? – for their stage show."

"Oh," I said, not wanting to encourage any further discussion or lame comedy.

The Chief pulled up within about ten yards of the semi. "Right there," he said and pointed. "You see what I mean?"

"I don't see anything," I said after I'd made a show of looking.

"The left corner of the fender. Look again."

96

I did as he directed me, but I still had no clue what he was talking about.

"Do you see the black paint smudged on it? It's as if it rubbed up against or ran into something that left that paint mark."

"That's an old truck, Chief. That could have been there for years."

"You know, that's exactly what I thought. So I took a sample and sent it up to an old academy buddy of mine at the F.B.I. lab in Toledo. He ran some tests for me and said that paint's an 'obsidian black metallic.'"

"Yeah?"

"Yeah. And he said it's a pretty rare color used mostly on recent model Mercedes Benz luxury vehicles."

The drum beat in my head switched from whole notes to sixteenth notes, for the direction of his line of conjecture had become abundantly clear.

"You okay, son? You're looking a little flushed. Would you like some water? I have some right here."

"Please," I said.

The Chief opened and reached into his center console and retrieved a bottle of water. "Anyway, that means that paint couldn't have been there but a year or two at the most. So I did some searching through our records at the station and couldn't find a single accident report involving Mr. Mooseburger and his semi."

"Maybe it happened somewhere out of town."

"I thought that too, but when I ran the plate through the system, it came up empty."

"Maybe he didn't report it, or someone hit him and ran."

"Now, you got me there. That might be it exactly."

I breathed a sigh of relief.

"But just for shits and giggles," the Chief resumed. "I started searching the data base for Mercedes Benz owners in and around Goodness Falls. You want to know what I found?"

"There aren't many Mercedes Benz owners in and around the village of Goodness Falls."

"That's right. You want to know how many?"

I didn't answer.

"Three," he said. "Exactly three. A red GL 350 SUV, a White SLK-55 Roadster, and an obsidian black metallic CLS 550 Coupe, registered to . . ."

"Dr. Stone," I finished his sentence.

"That's right again. Still, that alone doesn't prove a thing without a witness to place the Mercedes at the scene of the accident. He pulled out his little spiral notebook from his shirt pocket. "Let's see," the Chief said – he thumbed through the pages – "Here it is. It says right here. 'Dr. Stone and T.J. Farrell near scene of accident approx. 7:00 a.m. Saw nothing.'" He closed his notebook and stared through the windshield at the semi's bumper for what seemed a very long time. Finally, he asked, "Do you understand my concern, T.J.?"

"Yes, sir."

"But when I spoke to the Doctor, he insisted that he drove a red Cabriolet that day because his Mercedes was in a shop in Toledo, and he does have the title to such a vehicle; although, between the two of us, I'd never seen it around here before, and it seemed to be news to the Mrs. But she confirmed his ownership."

That meant that Dr. Stone must have been forced to come clean to his wife regarding his "friend" at the hospital. Like me, I'm sure Mrs. Stone figured she was better off with him free than in jail. Considering her expensive-to-maintain lifestyle, she wouldn't have been difficult to convince.

"I know you already told me that you didn't see anything unusual that morning. I just need you to confirm that Dr. Stone did, in fact, drive the two of you to Toledo and back in the red Cabriolet. If you can do that, we can put this baby to bed and chalk up that paint on the fender to being a mystery. If you can't, I'm going to need to chase down that Mercedes and check it for damage or recent body work. Whaddya say?"

For a moment, I was seriously tempted to cash in, tell the truth, and wash the guilt from off my soul, but I kept "my shit together" as Dr. Stone had warned me to do. "Yes, sir," I said. "We took the Cabriolet."

"Okay. Great. That's all I needed." The Chief made a quick note inside his notebook. "I appreciate your help, son."

"Can you take me home now?"

"Will do."

Chapter Twelve

Wednesday Night, October 31, 201_

My mom and Bo met me at the back door: Bo with his tail wagging, my mom with her tongue.

"Hey, boy," I bent over and rubbed behind Bo's ears.

"T.J.! What's the matter? Why did the Chief bring you home?" My mom peeked through the curtains in the window over the sink. "You're not in trouble are you, honey? Did he find out about the party at the Tuckers' place?"

"No, Mom. I'm not in trouble. The Chief just gave me a ride home."

"A ride home? Why didn't you call?"

"My cell battery died," I lied. "I was walking uptown to the diner to use their phone when the Chief pulled over and offered me a ride." I was in no mood to explain my fight with Caly to my mom.

"Wasn't that nice of the Chief?"

"Yeah."

"Are you hungry? You look pale. Would you like me to heat something up?"

"No. I'm good." I couldn't complain about the headache, or she might go looking for the Vicodin that was no longer in her medicine cabinet. "I'm just going to go up to my room. Maybe go to sleep early. C'mon, Bo."

"Wait," she stopped me. "Your dad's new employee orientation at the hospital is tomorrow. He'll be leaving early and taking the truck. You'll need to find a ride to school, or you can take the bus."

"The bus? Mom, I'm a senior."

"What about Caly?"

"I'll take care of it," I said, just wanting to end the conversation and not to discuss Caly.

"You've got to see your father, T.J. You're not going to believe it. You're not going to recognize him."

"Why's that? Is he standing up?"

She made no effort to mask the hurtfulness of my sarcasm. "Your father's a good man. It wouldn't kill you to show a little respect and to maybe show some faith in him."

I didn't have the energy for an argument, and the pain in my head was pushing an eight on the ten point pain scale. Besides, I didn't need the drama, so I said, "I'm sorry, Mom."

She perked right back up. "Stay here. I'll go get your father."

From habit more than hunger, I opened the refrigerator and bent over to study its typically disappointing contents.

"T.J." My mom said.

I stood up and turned around. Next to my mom stood a stranger. It was someone my dad used to be or someone he hoped to become. I wasn't sure because I'd never known the former, and I'd never imagined the latter. His hair was cut and combed and his face shaven. He wore a white, long sleeved, button-down work shirt with "Tom" sewn in blue script inside a blue-bordered, oval patch over his heart and "Toledo Medical Center" stitched inside a matching patch on the right side of his chest. On bottom, he wore brand new, blue, twill work pants and a pair of fresh-from-the-box, steel-toed work boots. He looked at least fifteen pounds lighter and two inches taller.

"Well, what do you think?" My dad said.

I didn't know what to say. I'd forever disassociated happy from home. I had to will myself not to cry, but I found it surprisingly easy to cross the kitchen and join my parents in a three-way embrace. In that moment, my head didn't hurt, and all of my worries over football, Caly, Dr. Stone, and the Chief went away, and I still believed I could work all of that out.

"I told you God was listening and things were going to go our way," my mom said.

With Bo at my feet, I sat in our tiny living room and watched the Wednesday night lottery drawing and *The Wheel of Fortune* with my mom and dad. Together we solved the puzzle for the phrase: "Don't count your chickens." It was the first time – in I couldn't remember how long – that I'd spent more than fifteen minutes in a room with either of them. However, there are no intimates more jealous or more demanding of our undivided attention than pain. Within an hour, mine was screaming in my ear, but without the pills, I had no way to pacify it.

"Can I use the truck to run to Caly's?" I asked.

My mom looked to my dad, who nodded. "Sure, honey, but don't stay too late. It's a school night."

"I won't," I said and strode out through the kitchen.

"Tell the Stones we said hello," my mom called as I shut the door behind me.

*****

I had no intention of going to the Stones. Instead, I was going to look for something to alleviate the pain in my head. I drove to the eastern edge of Goodness Falls' corporation limits and pulled into a driveway with large, reflective signs warning: "Private Property" and "No Trespassers. Violators Will Be Prosecuted." It was an old limestone quarry that'd been closed down for years. The signs were intended to cover the owners' asses – whoever they were.

Whereas the jock types at the high school and the so-called good kids claimed ownership to Resthaven for our partying purposes, the quarry belonged to the stoners. For the most part, the cops didn't bother us because they were all townies themselves, who had partied in Resthaven when they were kids.

The quarry was different. The cops got their rocks off and earned their pay by hassling those kids, most of whom came from families even more fucked up than mine. Few of their parents were even together. None of their parents were on village council or school board. Most of their parents didn't even vote, much less campaign in support of safety services tax levies. A lot of their parents had their own regular run-ins with the local cops for drug possession, drunk and disorderlies, failed child support, domestic abuse, etc.

I doused my headlights and took the gravel road to the right and around to the rear of the quarry, where I parked the pickup. I got out and walked over stones and through some brush until a deep pool of night-sky-reflecting quarry water appeared beneath me inside deeply-scarred limestone walls and precipitous cliffs. The pond was at least a football field in width and two in length. Here and there around the quarry's edges, I could see small fires and camp lanterns, and I could hear earnest voices on the breeze. I circled towards the right and the nearest source of light and sound.

As I drew near, occasional orange firings lit up then moved in a tight circle. Voices grew louder and indiscernible figures appeared huddled around a campfire.

"Hey," I said and sent the figures scurrying into the dark. "It's cool. I'm not the cops."

One-by-one, they stepped back inside the glow of their firelight.

"It's just me. T.J. Farrell," I said and stepped out of the blackness.

"What the fuck are you doing here, Farrell?"

I recognized the voice immediately. It was that of the only person I knew who might be able to provide relief for my pain. "Hey, Donny. I came to see you."

"Did my old man send you on some sort of intervention mission?" Since joining the stoner crowd, Donny Harris' voice had acquired an affected street tough's inflection.

His friends laughed at the notion.

"No. The Coach and I aren't exactly getting along too well right now either. Actually, he benched me."

"I heard that. Isn't that ironic?" Donny said. "Welcome to the club."

"Can I talk to you for a minute?" I asked.

"Free country," he answered.

"Privately?"

Donny made a show of being bothered but said, "Why not?" He stood up, passed the joint he'd been cupping in his palm to some girl next to him, and joined me outside the campfire light.

"S'up," Donny said and gave me a halfhearted bro handshake and one-armed hug. "You want me to talk to the Coach for you, bro?" He asked sarcastically.

"No. I think I can take care of that situation myself."

"You know, you ought to just say 'fuck it.' In a few weeks, the whole football hero horseshit will be over anyway. Then what? The only way you win, bro, is by quitting it before it quits on you. You know what I mean?"

"It's not that easy. I'm still hoping to play ball in college. The coach from Toledo is coming to the game Friday night to watch me play."

"It's your life. What can I do for you then? You looking for something to give you an edge? How about some Addies or some Vitamin-R?"

"I don't know what those are."

"Adderall, bro. And Ritalin. That shit will give you more focus and energy than any of my old man's lame pep talks."

"I need Vicodin," I blurted out.

"Vikes! Yikes!" Donny said and laughed at his doggerel. "I'm shocked. I didn't know Touchdown T.J. Farrell was that kind of playa. Who'd have thought?"

"I'm not. I just got a headache that won't quit."

"Another concussion?"

"Probably."

"How many is that?"

"I don't know. Officially, I've only had two. In reality, since the fourth grade, too many to count probably."

"Pain is temporary. Pride is forever," Donny mockingly quoted one of the inspirational signs prominently hung by his father in the football locker room.

"I've been taking my mom's pills, but they're all gone."

"Sorry, bro, but I can't help you. Vikes aren't hard to get, but they're hard as hell to hold on to – if you know what I mean."

I didn't.

"My advice to you is to start pharming," Donny said.

"Farming?"

"Yeah. Pharming with a "ph.""

"Pharming?"

"Bro," Donny grew impatient. "Where'd you steal your mom's Vikes?"

"From the medicine cabinet."

"That's right. That's pharming. Pharmaceuticals. You get it?"

Oh, pharming – with a ph."

"Right. But you've already harvested that field. Now you need to go over to a neighbor's house or a relative's or, better yet, that fine Caly Stone's house and do some pharming there. Shit! Her daddy is a doctor. You should pull in a bumper crop."

"I need it now," I said with the desperation of a burgeoning addict.

"Like I said, I ain't got it, but I have one of these." He reached into the pocket of his jeans and pulled out a plastic baggie with several already-rolled joints. "A little medical marijuana should help. It definitely won't hurt."

"I don't have any money on me."

"No problem, bro. I'll float you one."

"Thanks," I said and started to walk away. I stopped and turned around. "Hey, Donny."

"Yeah?"

"We never . . . I guess, I never talked about . . . you know . . . what happened."

"No need to. It's no big deal. I was never happier than the day my old man benched me. The father-son football thing was his dream, not mine. I hated that shit. I pretended pretty good all those years just to make him happy, but it ate me up inside. I'm happier hanging out with these fuck ups than I ever was in that locker room. They're my family now."

*****

After Donny returned to his friends, I sat in the bed of the Ranger and smoked the joint beneath the stars. It was nowhere near as effective as the Vicodin, but it at least succeeded at taking the edge off of the headache. In fact, it relaxed me so much that I dozed off. My sleep over the past few days had been erratic at best, so I was exhausted.

Sometime later, a pair of flickering high beams woke me up. I covered my eyes and shivered against the cold that had set in while I slept.

"Farrell," Donny's voice called from behind the blinding white lights of a jacked-up pickup. "You still here?"

I didn't bother to answer the obvious. Disoriented from the pot and still sleepy, I slipped my cell from my pocket and checked the time: 11:38. The door of the pickup slammed shut and Donny appeared in its beams. "As long as you're still here, bro, you want to go to a concert?"

"A concert? It's nearly midnight on a Wednesday. Where is there a concert now?"

"Christ, Farrell. You really are a cherry, aren't you?"

I rubbed my eyes and pulled my knees up against my chest. "I don't know what you mean."

"A cherry. Like a virgin."

I ignored the insult. "I'm only eighteen. I can't get into a club."

"This ain't at no club. And there won't be nobody checking ID's. It's an underground Halloween Bash, bro. Should be crazy."

"Where is it?"

"Can't tell you or I'd have to kill you."

"Funny."

"Just come with us. It's going to be bad ass. There's a sick death metal band from Toledo coming in. They're called Yorick. Crazy as shit, bro. Plus, I'll be able to hook you up with some Vikes for sure."

Donny must have seen my eyes light up at the mention of Mr. Mortis's band and/or the Vicodin.

"C'mon, bro. It's out past your place in Crystal Ridge at the old winery. We'll follow you. You can drop off your truck and get some cash for the party and pills."

We did exactly as Donny suggested. The lights were still on in the kitchen, where Bo met me with his tail wagging. My parents had already gone to bed, but according to our system, I was expected to peek my head in whenever I came home and they weren't up. I could hear my dad's snoring as I crossed the warped wooden floor boards of the living room and opened their bedroom door just enough to stick my face through.

"Mom?" I whispered. "Mom?" I whispered louder.

"Huh? What?" She sat up and asked.

"It's me, Mom. I'm home. You can go back to sleep. I'll see you in the morning."

"Okay, honey. You're a good boy," she said and was back to sleep before her head settled into her pillow. My dad never moved.

I let Bo out to take care of his business for the evening, but he didn't like anything about Donny and his friends being parked in the driveway. He let them know with a showing of his teeth and a series of warning barks.

"C'mon, Bo," I said. I grabbed him by his collar and led him towards the barn. After he'd finished, I walked him back inside and up to my room, where he lay down at the foot of my bed. "Good boy," I praised him and rubbed him behind the ears and on his belly. He whimpered when he realized I wasn't staying. I closed the door behind me, so Bo couldn't rat me out to my folks.

On my way out through the kitchen, I shook down Winnie-the-Pooh for three twenty dollar bills from the Zip-loc bag at the bottom of the jar in which my mom hid her Christmas money. She'd been stashing it there for years, but I'd never before dared to tap into it. But the pounding was increasing in severity inside my head. I badly needed the Vicodin. I figured the money would eventually go towards me anyway, so I was just borrowing against myself.

Donny sat in the shotgun seat. The truck belonged to Dusty Kearns. Like Donny, he graduated the previous year. He had been in the Vo-Ag program, so I'd never shared any classes with him or even saw him around school much. His family owned one of the largest soybean farms in the county, so he pretty much had it made. "S'up?" Dusty said, as I slid into the backseat and checked out my fellow passengers.

"Holy shit!" I screamed and jumped back out of the door to the accompaniment of everyone's laughter.

"It's Halloween, bro," Donny said. "They're zombies. Get in."

I recognized the zombie next to the window as the gravedigger from the men's room at the church.

"Hey! I know this dude," the Gravedigger announced, but he was clearly tripping on something, so everyone ignored his declaration, including me. It had been his costume that had scared the shit out of me. He was big like Moose and dressed like him in soiled work clothes: Wranglers, work boots, and a plaid flannel shirt. He had a fake gaping wound across his forehead, blackened eyes, fake blood oozing from his nose, and some kind of snaggletooth mouthpiece. All of which made him look a lot like Moose's ghost.

The zombie in the middle was a girl, and despite the pasty makeup, the fake blood dripping from the corner of her mouth, and what looked like a maggot-infested splotch in her black wig, she reminded me of a hot, younger version of Miss Havisham from Dickens' *Great Expectations*. She was all but busting out of a low-cut, ripped and yellowed wedding dress, which she wore over a pair of incongruous black combat boots. On her lap rested a bouquet of dry, crinkly, and withered black roses. Donny introduced them both, but Dusty had cranked up the radio so that I couldn't hear a word Donny said.

I couldn't tell if the Gravedigger and Miss Havisham were a couple or not. But he repeatedly snuck peeks down her dress, and she did little to prevent him from enjoying the view.

Dusty exited my driveway quietly, but as soon as we were on Hill Road and pointed north toward the bay, he hit the gas. The engine roared. Where Hill Road met the bay waters, there was a wicked, right-angled bend in the road, which locals predictably called Dead Man's Curve. At that point, Hill became Bayshore Road. On the inland side of the curve was where the dreaded Daltons lived. About two miles down from their property sat the old Crystal Ridge Winery on over two-hundred acres of once-cultivated vineyards overrun by wild grapes. It was Erie County's most notoriously-haunted location.

During the winery's heyday, the grapes were pressed and processed into wine in an outbuilding at the back of the property that had long ago burned to the ground. A number of migrant workers burned to death in the fire. They say that, if you listen closely on Halloween night, you can hear them screaming in Spanish.

A small hill, more like a mound really, rose in the center of the property. On top of the hill was what was once the main building of the winery with a wine store and gift shop on the first level. All that remained of that stone structure, however, was what amounted to jagged ruins, but underneath, built into the hillside, was a massive wine cellar, where the wine casks were once stored inside its cool confines and where the night's rock concert/Halloween bash was being held.

From the road, there was no sign of any life on the winery property.

"Are you sure you've got the right place?" I screamed at Donny over the music.

"Trust me, bro," he said as Dusty pulled into a long, twisting driveway. A dilapidated, porcelain sign in the shape of an arrow pointed the way towards the old store. A little farther along the serpentine course, Donny said, "Look," and he pointed down at the grass near the side of the driveway. Another arrow, this one formed from multi-colored glow sticks, confirmed that we were in the right location. As we neared the ruins on the hill, a single sawhorse blockaded the way, and Dusty was forced to hit the brakes.

A long-haired freak, wearing a top hat, a Guy Fawkes mask, and a black trench coat, suddenly appeared at Donny's rolled down window. "Cut the lights," a deep voice, muffled by the mask commanded. "You guys going somewhere?" He asked through the painted-on smile of the mask.

"We're looking for the concert, bro," Donny explained.

Guy Fawkes shined a flashlight around the inside of the truck. He took his time running its beam the length of the zombified Miss Havisham's body then came to a complete and suspicious stop on me still in my thrift shop skater clothes. "Who's this dude?"

"A friend," Donny answered. "He's cool."

Guy Fawkes didn't seem convinced but he accepted Donny's endorsement. "No weapons of any kind inside. Not even wallet chains. Any of you strapping?"

"No, we're cool." Donny said.

"How about *The Walking Dead* chick. She hiding anything up under that dress? Maybe I should feel her up."

Miss Havisham didn't flinch. With her eyes unblinkingly locked on Guy Fawkes, she coolly reached down, gathered her layers of wedding dress in a bundle, lifted her ass off the seat, and pulled the dress up over her waist, exposing a black garter and black panties to match her boots but no weapons. After pausing long enough to allow the five of us guys to pick our jaws off of our chests and to adjust our suddenly snug jeans, Miss Havisham pulled her skirts back down. "Satisfied?" She asked.

"Twenty bucks a piece for the band and to cover expenses," Guy Fawkes said, apparently more than satisfied.

We all passed our bills to Donny who paid the man.

"There's another arrow up ahead. Follow it around to the back of the hill. You can park there."

There had to be a hundred cars and trucks in the gravel lot. Near the door, I recognized Mr. Mortis's black sport wagon. The earth around the cellar made for a very effective muffler, for as we approached the entrance, I couldn't hear a note or noise coming from inside. We descended six concrete steps inside a narrow staircase lit only by a single red bulb. At the bottom of the stairs stood a heavy metal door. When we opened it, we were overwhelmed by a tidal wave of smoke, sound, and body heat. Drums pounded and guitars thrashed at breakneck speeds as what sounded like a demon's guttural roar spewed from the lead singer's mouth in his attempt to at least be heard, if not understood, over the band.

A few overhead bulbs inside metal cages hung from conduit in the low ceiling, but the bulbs struggled to penetrate the tomblike and palpable darkness inside the wine cellar. The space could only be navigated by touch and by slipping through the occasional spaces between bodies illuminated by the stage lights. It took us ten minutes to push, shove, and weasel our way to within ten feet or so of the band, primarily lit in blood red spotlights and the occasional flashings of lightning-white strobes, which transformed the band's hypnotic and otherwise maniacal playing and head banging into slow motion and reflected off of the chrome skulls, scrap metal, and silver inverted crucifixes which decorated the stage.

The moshing-room-only crowd surged and swayed in communal catharsis. Other than Miss Havisham, in the darkness and among the preponderance of black clothed and long-haired partiers (many in costume), it was difficult to discern male from female. I'd guess there were at least five dicks for every chick. The space oozed testosterone.

Despite the dark themes and tone of the music and the funereal dress of the congregation, I felt no threat of violence. In fact, I felt the opposite. I felt part and parcel of a living organism whose unique cells had coalesced for one evening in a unified and symbiotic form that would never again be regenerated in that exact configuration. The feeling was simultaneously masturbatory and orgiastic. Even the pain and suffering in my head seemed to meld with that being expressed through the music and being released by those faithlessly gathered. It was as if the band and crowd had assumed my misery as its own and, in so doing, absorbed, dispersed,   and abated the pain's power over me.

Although he screamed at the top of his voice, I felt Donny's lips brush my ear before I actually heard his words. "I'll be right back," he said then disappeared into the pandemonium.

I smiled and nodded my confirmation of his message rather than even attempting to make my voice heard. I was more-than-happy to remain where I stood. My and Miss Havisham's bodies were being increasingly pressed into one another. After our fight in the cemetery, I had no idea what my status was with Caly nor, in what had become to seem more dream than reality inside that wine cellar, did I care if I was being in any way unfaithful. I felt more alive amongst those death metal worshippers than at any point I could remember.

Miss Havisham yelled something towards me as we involuntarily bumped and grinded against one another. Looking down at the top of her head, in the crazy lighting, the maggots – which I assumed actually to be white rice – occasionally seemed to wriggle.

"What?" I asked and leaned my ear towards her mouth.

"I know the guitarist." She pointed in the direction of Mr. Mortis.

"Me too," I screamed down to her. "He's my English teacher."

"He's my uncle," she one-upped me.

"No way!" I yelled and returned my attention to the stage.

Mr. Mortis tore into a wicked guitar solo. He appeared completely transfixed by his own performance and totally oblivious to our presence. When he finished, he offhandedly flicked his guitar pick into the crowd. Mesmerized, Miss

Havisham and I watched its slow flight through flashing strobes. Somehow, it managed to soar through the many upraised hands and fingers, formed in the shape of the devil's horns, like an extra point kicked through a line of goal posts. In the moment prior to striking my forehead, it banked sharply to the right and plunked the Gravedigger over the ear. I turned to Miss Havisham and laughed.

She seemed surprised by the guitar pick's target.

"Farrell," Donny's voice wormed into my consciousness from the side opposite of Miss Havisham. "I hooked you up." First, he handed me a tall shot glass of something that tasted like black licorice but went down smoothly, then he slipped what appeared to be a wad of foil into my palm. "Twenty bucks, bro. I got you a parachute."

"A what?" I asked confusedly.

"Just swallow it. Trust me."

I assumed he wasn't asking me to swallow a foil ball. It had to be my Vicodin. I dug another of my mom's twenties from my pocket and traded Donny. Inside the foil was a wad of ultra-thin, single-ply Kleenex or toilet paper in the tear drop shape and size of a Hershey Kiss. The Vicodin had been pulverized into a dust and was contained inside the tissue. Once more, I looked suspiciously at Donny.

"Swallow it, bro. You'll forget you ever had a headache. Shit, you'll forget you were ever alive."

I did as he suggested.

He was right.

As the parachute unraveled, time passed in a blur. I vaguely remember being repeatedly knocked back and forth between the Gravedigger and Miss Havisham by the non-stop moshing. I remember her climbing on top of and sitting on my shoulders, from where she squeezed her surprisingly cold thighs tightly around my cheeks. I remember the Gravedigger and I picking her up and passing her nearly weightless body to the guys in front of us. From there, she crowd surfed, face down, from one set of grateful hands to another until she beached on stage and thrashed around next to Mr. Mortis like a girl possessed until she dived back into the sea of death metal acolytes and returned to her position between the Gravedigger and myself. I remember her reaching up and grabbing him by his shirt front, pulling his mouth down to hers, and giving him a tonsil-deep kiss while waves of disappointment and envy washed through me.

The next thing I recall is the Gravedigger keeling over and falling to the floor.

"Adios, gaucho," Miss Havisham turned to me and said.

"Perdita?"

The name hadn't completely passed my lips before I was suddenly displaced in the opposite direction by a body much larger than my own slamming into me.

As the blob-like mob tried to re-absorb me, she turned and began to snake her way in the other direction toward the exit. I lunged for her shoulder. My fingers became entangled in the synthetic strands of her wig, which came off in my hand and allowed her to escape. Like Prince Charming holding Cinderella's slipper, I held the wig and studied it. The puddle of maggots was apparently not a part of the costume.

The Vicodin parachute suddenly and fully deployed. It jerked me out of any consciousness of reality, and I have no memory of the time that immediately followed.

*****

I don't know how or when, but at some point, I reunited with Donny and his friends minus Miss Havisham, who I didn't see again that night. I vaguely remember a long ride in Dusty's truck with the Gravedigger moaning in the backseat next to me and Donny exhorting Dusty to "Hurry, bro!"

Later, I found myself standing on uncertain feet on my back porch while Donny worked my house key into the lock and me through the mud room and into the kitchen.

Whimpering, Bo met me at my bedroom door. The red, digital numbers on my alarm clock read 4:13 a.m. I pulled the curtains tight across my bedroom window and threw a stray towel over the red digital numbers on my alarm clock which were penetrating my skull like laser beams. My buzz was diminishing fast and the headache was returning with a vengeance. As Donny promised, the parachute method had provided a faster-acting relief from the pain, but it was also shorter-lived. The parachute was about to touch down – hard. Maintaining total darkness and keeping my head completely motionless on my pillow were the only available remedies at my disposal to diminish the impact.

Chapter Thirteen

Thursday Morning, November 1, 201_

From somewhere beyond the tomb-like blackness, an irritatingly familiar voice called my name. It demanded, "Get out of bed!" It also warned that I was going to be late for something. However, I couldn't imagine anyplace I wanted to be other than inside that house, inside my bedroom, inside those covers, inside a space insulated by sleep against the pain that waited for me outside of my sleep, covers, bedroom, and house.

"Teeee.Jaaaay! You got to get up." The voice registered as my mom's.

Reluctantly, I rose from the depths toward the murky light. I broke the surface of consciousness and slowly acclimated myself to shared reality. I reached over and removed the towel from over the alarm clock: seven o'clock. I had no idea how long I'd been sleeping. For all I knew, it could have been a day; it could have been a minute. I stared at the clock, but I couldn't remember if the damn dot in the corner signified a.m. or p.m.

"You're going to be late for school!" The infernal voice warned.

A.M.

I'd been sleeping for less than three hours.

Sensing my wakefulness, Bo had already positioned himself at the door. He whimpered to warn me that he needed to get outside fast.

Still wearing the clothes from the day before, I extended my reach as far as I could without actually getting out of bed. My fingers got just enough of the knob to rotate it and sling the door open. Bo abandoned me immediately to Nature's call and slipped out the door and down the stairs into the kitchen, where my mom mercifully let him outside. I lost my balance, fell to the floor in a thud, and lay there contentedly.

"T.J.?" My mom called and summoned me to the surface once again. "Is everything okay up there?"

"I'm fine. I'll be down in a minute," I said, but I was far from fine. My head felt like a fractured egg shell. I couldn't imagine how I was going to make it through an entire school day without pills. I tried to convince myself that it was a good thing, that I was being weak and becoming too dependent on them anyway. It was time to get tough, to man up, and to play through the pain. Basically, I repeated every banality I'd been fed by my coaches during eight years of organized football: "No pain; no gain!" "Pain is temporary. Pride is forever." "When the going gets tough, the tough get going." The cumulative weight of them wasn't even remotely as effective as a half a Vicodin would have been.

"Don't forget," my mom called once more, "you need to find a ride to school or take the bus. Your dad started his new job today. Isn't that exciting?" The unadulterated joy she was experiencing on the first day of her new life was obvious. I should have been happy for her, but the only thing I could think about was the head-splitting pain.

I texted Scags, who answered that he'd pick me up in ten minutes, which didn't leave me much time to get ready, but the mere thought of water from the shower pelting me in the head was more than I could bear anyway. I didn't bother to change my clothes. In the way of grooming, I did no more than run my fingers through my hair as I staggered down the stairs, and my shadow-beard was well past five o'clock.

"Aren't you going to clean up, honey?" My mom asked.

"There's no time. I overslept. Scags is on his way."

"At least eat something," my mom bargained. "I'll make you toast." She was up in an instant sliding open and slamming shut bread drawers and silverware drawers. Each bang of cabinetry and clang of knives, forks, and spoons was an assault on my ears and head.

"Mom! Stop! I'm not hungry."

"You got to eat," she said, ignoring my insolent tone and continuing to gather margarine and jelly from the refrigerator, the bright light from which fried my brain. She yapped on and on about my dad's job and something about new curtains, but I was unable to focus on her rambling. Mercifully, my phone buzzed in my pocket with a text from Scags announcing his arrival.

"I've got to go. My ride's here." I was up and out of my chair before she could finish spreading the grape jelly on the bread. The back door closed behind me and on her extended, toast-filled hands.

"You look like death warmed over," Scags said as I climbed into his red Ford F-150.

"What does that even mean?" I asked.

"My mom says it all the time. I didn't know what it meant myself until just now."

"It's just a touch of flu or something," I said by way of explanation.

"I'd say it's more than a touch. You look like you've been raped by the flu."

"Whatever. Let's just go. And stop by the Get-Go. I need an energy drink."

"Or ten," Scags punctuated my sentence.

*****

"Hey, did you hear about the stabbing?" Scags asked after we'd returned to his truck and were once again en route to school.

"What are you talking about?"

"There was some kind of Halloween party at the old winery last night," Scags explained. "Some dude got stabbed."

"Who? Who was it?" I was suddenly interested.

"I don't know him. He didn't live around here. I guess he'd just started working at the cemetery. The crazy part is that he was dressed like a zombie, so I guess – for a long time – no one even knew he'd been stabbed. They assumed the blood was part of his costume."

"The Gravedigger," I said more to myself than Scags.

"What?"

"You're shitting me," I said.

"I shit you not. And, when he went down, everyone figured he was just drunk or high. They left him lying there and partied right around him. It wasn't until the party was over that anyone realized that the guy had been stabbed and was bleeding out on the floor."

"Is he dead?"

"All I know is someone dropped him off at the emergency room entrance and left him."

"How do you know all of this?"

"It's all over Twitter."

"Fuck me," I said.

"Right?" Scags said clueless of my intimate association with the events he'd just described. "They're dropping like flies around here all of a sudden. It's like someone dropped a curse on Goodness Falls."

We were on our way to first period math when I told Scags to go on ahead and that I'd catch up to him. I detoured to the guidance office, where I'd been a volunteer aide as a junior and had grown pretty close to the secretary.

Mrs. Martinez was beautiful. I mean Jennifer Lopez beautiful with mocha-colored skin and long, honey-blond hair with golden highlights that looked as if it were constantly being wind-blown – even inside the windowless office, where she sat with an impressive amount of cleavage exposed over the plunging neckline of a brown and orange, form-fitting dress. Beneath her desk, I noticed one open-toed, beige, high-heeled sandal on the planted foot of her crossed legs – far-from-the-most-practical choice of footwear. Somehow she looked simultaneously *over*dressed and *under*dressed for a high school guidance secretary, as if she could easily leave school and head directly to the club.

"Mira quien acaba de llegar," Mrs. Martinez greeted me when she finally looked up from the envelopes she was stuffing.

"I don't know what that means, Mrs. Martinez, but I'm pretty sure it's not good."

"Look who the cat dragged in is what it means. You look terrible, T.J., and you don't smell so good either."

"It's been a rough morning."

"You're the talk around the school."

"I am?"

"People are saying that you may not play tomorrow night and that you and Caly Stone broke up."

"Don't worry. I've got it all under control."

"Do you? It don't look like you do. What you here for? You need to see a counselor? Maybe, you want to talk about your friend Moose. You look like you could use a counselor. Let me see if . . ." She started to rise from her desk to check if either one of the counselors was available.

"No. I'm good," I said. The last thing I needed was a counselor putting one of her half-ass, grief counseling or drug awareness in-service workshops to work on me. "I came to see you, Mrs. Martinez. I need a favor."

"A favor? What kind of favor?"

"Could you look up some information for me on a student? She's a new kid I met at Moose's funeral. I thought I could maybe help her fit in faster, you know? If you could tell me her class schedule, I wouldn't have to run around hoping to bump into her."

"Is this new girl why you and Caly are broken up?"

"No. And we're not broken up. We just had a fight. That's all."

"What's this girl's name?"

"All I know is her first name: Perdita."

"The lost one. La perdida."

"What's that?" I asked.

"It's Spanish. Perdida means 'the lost one,' but I don't remember enrolling a student by that name."

"She just moved to town. She may even be one of the migrant kids."

Mrs. Martinez continued to scroll through computerized records but came up empty. "Sorry, T.J. There's no one registered by that name."

I didn't know what to think.

"Is there anything else? You sure you don't want to talk to someone? It would do you good."

"No. I'm fine. Thanks, Mrs. Martinez." I suddenly had a second thought. "There is one more thing. What do you know about Mr. Mortis?"

Mrs. Martinez's expression turned grave. "I don't know nothing about him, and I do not want to know." Oddly, she executed a speedy sign of the cross to the jangling accompaniment of a half –dozen gold bracelets that slid up and down her forearm.

The bell rang to signal the beginning of the first period, but my head was still pounding along with the still-echoing, frenetic bass lines of Yorick. I couldn't bear the thought of going to class. Instead, I headed for the nurse's office, played the flu card, and convinced her to allow me to lie down on the single cot in a small infirmary adjacent to her office. After checking my records, she dispensed a couple of worthless Tylenol and directed me to the windowless infirmary no bigger than a walk-in closet; however, it provided soothing warmth and darkness. For the next few hours, I didn't sleep so much as I floated in and out of a dreamless half-consciousness. It was nearly eleven when the nurse stuck her head in the door and woke me. "You should go home. Let me call your mother," she said.

"No. I can't. If I go home, I can't practice. Coach's rule is no practice, no play."

The bell rang to signal the beginning of the first lunch period. It was Caly's lunch. I needed to see her, feel out where we stood, and once more start to patch things up.

"Let me try to eat something. Maybe I'll feel better." I pleaded with the nurse and she reluctantly agreed.

"You can freshen up if you'd like," she said and nodded towards a white porcelain sink against the wall in her outer office.

As I bent over to wash my face and hands, a student dressed in gym shorts and a t-shirt rushed into the office. Apparently, some kid had fallen in P.E. class and hit his head on the gymnasium floor. The nurse was needed immediately. I saw her hesitation to leave me alone, but my face and hands were wet and covered with soap. She turned the doorknob to a locked position with a key on the lanyard hanging from her neck. "Pull the door shut behind you when you go, and be quick about it," the nurse said before hurrying out of her office with an emergency first aid kit in her hand.

"Yes, M'am," I said, but as soon as I had dried off, I began pharming. I rummaged through the office for anything more powerful than the Tylenol. In a desk drawer, which had been inadequately shut to engage its lock, I found a single key labeled "Medicine Cabinet." On the wall hung a double door, metal cabinet whose tiny lock matched the key I'd found. Bottle after bottle of pills for menstrual pain relief lined the shelves. A shitload of ADHD drugs were stored there as well. With time running out before the nurse's return, I plucked a half-filled pill bottle from the bottom shelf. Even through the amber colored plastic of the bottle, I recognized the shape of the Vicodin tablets inside. A local dentist's name was on the label that also identified a classmate who had recently had all four wisdom teeth extracted. I was tempted to take the entire bottle and run, but I knew that would be unwise. Instead, I poured out four of the tablets, stuffed them in my pocket, and returned the bottle to its exact space on the shelf. After I'd closed and locked the medicine cabinet, I did the same with the key inside the desk drawer.

I heard the Nurse's voice approaching as I pulled her office door shut behind me and disappeared into the rush of students hurrying to lunch. En route, I stopped at a drinking fountain and threw back all four pills.

When I arrived in the cafeteria, Caly was already at the cheerleader table, where she sat with her back turned and next to Pete Terwilliger. I couldn't believe it! I swear. I tried to stay calm. I tried not to overreact. It may have been completely innocent. It probably was. I'm sure it was. But I couldn't control the rage that spontaneously combusted inside of me and erupted like a volcano. The prick had already been given my position; I wasn't about to let him take my girl and my future as well. I made a beeline for Terwilliger, placed him in a one-armed chokehold from behind, and began pulling him clean off his bench seat until I felt a hand on each of my biceps grasping me firmly from behind.

"Let him go, T.J." A commanding and familiar voice spoke directly into my ear. I didn't need to turn around. I knew Coach McKuen's voice better than my own dad's. He was on lunch duty. He must have seen the look in my eyes and read the intent on my face and followed me. "What the hell's wrong with you?" He added.

Through a madman's eyes, I glanced at the faces of those seated at Caly's table and at those nearby. In their minds, the jury was still out as to whether I was being serious and as to what my intentions may have been. As far as they knew, it may have been nothing more than typical guy behavior. It hadn't escalated far enough to be considered a fight, which would have meant my immediate suspension from school and from the game. Only Coach McKuen saw and only Terwilliger felt my malevolence – and Caly. She'd already witnessed and grown familiar with my newly-unleashed dark side on several occasions that week. Her eyes communicated her fear. She rose from her seat and hurried tearfully from the cafeteria with two girlfriends in pursuit.

"Let him go and walk with me, T.J." Coach McKuen said, "before you do something you'll regret for the rest of your life." The funny thing is if he'd have let me just beat the shit out of Terwilliger right then and there and get suspended, I may have gotten help and maybe I wouldn't be in here. Maybe I wouldn't be the most hated person in Goodness Falls. But I can't blame him. He thought he was doing me and everyone else a favor.

I released my hold. Terwilliger coughed a few times and the purple flushed from his face. "What's the matter with you, Farrell?!"

Before I could answer, Coach McKuen swung me around and walked me out of the cafeteria into an adjacent hallway, where I stormed back and forth venting my anger at Terwilliger, Caly, and pretty much the entire world.

"T.J.!" Coach McKuen finally grew tired of my shenanigans. "That's enough! And that," he pointed back towards the cafeteria, "was no way to handle being benched. I know you're pissed off. I don't like it either, but that's Coach Harris's call. So either accept it or do something about it with your play on the field. Fighting Terwilliger at school won't solve your problem. It'll only make it worse. Do you understand me?"

"Yes, sir," I said unconvincingly while I continued to pace.

"For now, you need to do what's best for the team. We can't afford this kind of horseshit heading into the playoffs."

"We can't afford to have me on the bench either. Tell Coach Harris that," I said with a completely inappropriate finger pointed at Coach McKuen's face.

"Trust me, I'd like to," he betrayed his sympathetic leanings, "but no one can tell him anything." After a brief pause, Coach McKuen asked, "What's your next class?"

"English."

"Go on and get there. And stay away from Terwilliger for the rest of the day."

"I will," I promised.

*****

Although he'd had no more, maybe even less sleep than I did, Mr. Mortis showed no ill effects of the previous night's bash. "T.J. Farrell in the flesh," he said, as I walked past him at the podium.

"More tragedy today, Mr. Mortis?" I asked in a snide tone.

"It's what I do," he answered coolly.

At least the Vicodin began to circulate through my system and to ease what had become the near-constant pain in my head. For the greater part of the period, I struggled to stay attentive to Mr. Mortis's lecture on the final scenes of *Macbeth* until I heard him recite, "'Lay on, Macduff, and be damned him who first cries 'Hold! Enough.'"

My interest was piqued.

"It is without question that, throughout the play, Macbeth has been victimized both by fate and his own poor and prideful choices," Mr. Mortis commented. "However, as evidenced by this line, at least *he* is not a quitter."

Mr. Mortis looked right at me. I swear he had emphasized the "he" for my benefit.

"Even though his death is both imminent and inevitable," Mr. Mortis continued, "Macbeth is able to gain a small measure of redemption through his determination to die well and his refusal to surrender his royal position without a fight, without at least some final act of defiance toward his enemies."

His words completely contradicted Coach McKuen's opposite advice to accept my demotion to second string. It caused me to question my unmanly willingness to step aside and to surrender my position (and my girlfriend) to Terwilliger, but it was already Thursday and time was running out.

After the last bell, Caly surprised me at my locker. Her cheerful attire of red, skinny stretch pants and a light blue button-down blouse beneath a navy blue, v-neck sweater didn't match her glum expression. To avoid being swept away by the stream of raucously exiting students, she leaned heavily against the bank of lockers. A brown cardboard box sat at her feet. Her arms were crossed beneath her chest and her chin was pressed against her sternum, which caused her hair to fall forward and curtain her face. Despite Caly's body language and the fact that the tide had begun to turn in the battle between the Vicodin and my headache back in favor of the pain, my heart and hopes soared at the sight of her.

"Hey! What's in the box?" I asked, but before she could even answer, I began to apologize for my behavior at lunch. "I'm really sorry about that thing with Pete and for losing my temper in the cemetery. With Moose and losing my starting position and worrying about the scholarship, I just haven't been myself lately, but it's going to be okay. I'm going to get it together and work all of it out. I promise."

"It's too late."

"What? What's 'too late'? It can't be too late. I can do this. You'll see. I'll talk to Coach. He's got to play me. He can't ruin this for me, for us."

"Teege," she lifted her chin from off her chest and tried to interrupt me.

"Maybe your dad can talk to Coach Harris. He's done it before."

"Teege! *This* is about my dad. He said I can't see you anymore."

"But . . . he told me he wanted me to be wherever you are . . . and that he needs to make me a 'suitable husband and son-in-law.' He told me that he could get me that scholarship." The strobes began to flash behind my eyes. I could feel my fists clenching and unclenching and my fingernails digging into my palms. "And you . . . you said that you 'had my back.' Remember? You said . . ."

"T.J.! Stop! Just . . . stop."

It dawned on me that she had chosen her time and location for the ambush carefully and well. She didn't want a scene or to give me a chance to confront her alone. If she were blunt with her words and unbending in her determination to break up with me, in the chaos of the senior hallway, she knew she could avoid both possibilities.

"That was before," she said. "Before you started talking and acting crazy. I don't even know you anymore." Caly hesitated then added, "You scare me."

Between being jostled by book bags carelessly slung over the shoulders of fleeing classmates, I glimpsed into the box positioned on the floor between us and recognized Valentine's and birthday cards I'd given her. There was a grey "Ducks Pride" t-shirt she'd literally taken off my back one summer day when we'd been swimming in Resthaven. She'd sworn to sleep in it every night. The stuffed pig I'd won her at the ring toss game at the previous summer's Erie County Fair lay on its side. Worst of all, my class ring, still on its chain, lay on the bottom. I reached into the box, removed it, and allowed it to dangle between my fingers.

"Caly," I pleaded.

"Do you have mine?" She asked bluntly.

"Caly," I said once more.

"Please, T.J. Don't make this harder." She held out her hand and tried to stifle a sniffle. I saw the tears rolling over her cheeks. "Please," she begged once more. The fast-diminishing flow of passersby was making her uncomfortable and impatient.

I removed the ring from inside of my t-shirt and pulled it up and over my head. "Are you sure?" I asked. "Can't we talk about this?"

"Please!" She stomped her foot in frustration and opened the dam for the tears to fall in torrents.

"Is everything okay out here?" Mr. Lamb stepped out of his classroom and asked.

"It's cool, Mr. Lamb," I said. "We're just talking."

Mr. Lamb gave a dubious look, but he stepped back inside his classroom, leaving his door open behind him.

I returned my attention to Caly and dangled the ring over her palm. "Always?" I asked hopefully. But I received no answering "and forever." Lightly, I set the ring down with the chain reluctantly following, draping, and folding itself over it.

Caly resisted all temptation to look into my eyes. She snapped shut her hand, spun on her red high heels, and half-ran down the hallway. I watched in stunned silence until she turned the corner that led to the main hall and out the front door of the high school.

"You coming?" A voice asked me from behind.

"What?" I turned to see Scags standing with his equipment bag draped over his shoulder.

"You need a ride to practice or what?"

I tried desperately to register what exactly had just happened with Caly and what our break up meant to my future and scholarship chances, but it was too much to process in the degenerated mush of my brain. Instead, I flipped it over to auto-pilot. I decided to go to practice as usual and think as little as possible until I could get a better handle on the situation and come up with a plan.

"Yeah," I answered and followed Scags out the rear entrance to where his truck was parked in the student lot.

*****

Prior to practice, I sat with Scags on the bench in front of his locker. We shared the special, playoff edition of the "Focus on Football" pull-out section of the local newspaper, *The Sandusky Reporter*. A two-page spread was devoted to Friday's rematch with Lakeview. The headline read: "Q.B. Change at Goodness Falls." A photograph, taken way back in August, showed me in my right-handed throwing stance posed back-to-back with the left-handed Terwilliger. The reporter cited "sources close to the team" as revealing Coach Harris's intention to start Terwilliger against Lakeview due to "undisclosed medical concerns regarding Farrell." The article declared that "Coach Harris should be applauded for placing the health concerns of his players over the desire to win."

I wanted to puke.

In one fluid movement, I stood, twirled, crumpled up the paper, and threw a perfect pass to the trash bin stationed near the door just as Coach Harris entered the locker room. He looked at me for a second, perhaps wondering if the projectile had been intended for him. He removed the wadded up newspaper from the bin, unfolded it, scanned the headline, and correctly interpreted my response to the article and my benching.

"Farrell!" He barked. "In my office. Now!"

"After he'd dismissed his assistants, he stood nose-to-nose with me and glared into my increasingly vacant eyes.

"Terwilliger *is* going to be my starting quarterback tomorrow night and for the remainder of the playoffs. Do I make myself clear?"

"Yes, sir," I said. "But Dr. Stone . . ."

"Don't you worry about Dr. Stone. We've already talked. Turns out I'd misjudged the man. He's arranged a little sit down after the game for me with Coach Markinson, who thinks he may have an open position on his staff next year after all."

I was too stunned to respond. How could Caly's father have betrayed me like that? Even more, how could he risk alienating me, the one person who knew the truth of his responsibility for Mr. Mooseburger's accident?

Then it hit me like a middle linebacker to the mouth. "You blackmailed him. Didn't you?"

"I don't know what you're talking about, Farrell."

"Last Saturday. The day of the accident. You followed me to the door of the locker room and waved to Dr. Stone. You . . ."

"Saw the Mercedes? Yes, I did, but I'd forgotten until the Chief came around asking questions."

"I'll tell," I said sounding like a child. "I'll tell Chief Johnson about the Mercedes myself."

"You go right ahead, but from what I understand, you've already told him that Dr. Stone picked you up in . . . let's see . . . a red Cabriolet was it? Now I'm no lawyer, but between that hit to the head last Friday night, your erratic behavior ever since, and my and Dr. Stone's testimony to the contrary of yours, I don't think you'd make for a very believable witness. Actually, I'd go so far as to suggest that your word isn't worth two shits around here right about now."

"I can't believe it," I said more to myself than Coach Harris.

"Well," he answered anyway, "you better believe it. Now, here's how it's going to be: I'll allow you to practice and to continue to dress out for the games, but you have taken your last snap for me. I wouldn't want you to hurt that pretty little head of yours."

I shook my head in disbelief of how much I'd lost in less than a week.

"I believe this whole thing is what the literary types, like that freak, Mr. Mortis, might call a tragedy."

Macbeth's words, as recited earlier in the week by Mr. Mortis, came back to me in perfect clarity: "A tale told by an idiot." I spoke them in a barely audible tone.

"What you call me?" Coach Harris asked with his dander up.

"Nothing," I responded. "I didn't say anything."

"By the way, I'm also red-flagging you for any recruiter who may still be willing to take a chance on your sorry ass and punch drunk head. When I'm finished spreading the word, you'll be lucky to get a grant-in-aid to play badminton from some division three, liberal arts college in Iowa much less a full ride to Toledo."

"Is that all, Coach?" I asked. "I need to get out to practice."

Coach Harris studied my expression, searched for signs of sarcasm or insolence, then said, "Get out of my sight."

*****

Practice was light with no contact and short, no more than a rehearsal of the game plan with a quick run through of offensive plays and defensive alignments, followed by a special teams period. After practice, I wrestled with the temptation to march into the coaches' office and to tell them all to "fuck off." The only thing that stopped me was the unwillingness to give Coach Harris the satisfaction of running me off.

I sat at my locker with the pain factory inside my head running at full capacity and watched the childish antics of my teammates. Most of the upperclassmen were singing and playing grab ass in the showers – the sophomores waited their turn out of deference and in the sheer terror of being harassed in some unimaginable manner by the bigger, stronger, and more sexually aggressive and deviant seniors, who seemed to have forgotten how, just two years prior, they had cowered in the same petrified manner as their current victims. Some of the guys stood around, talking nonchalantly in various stages of undress as only young men, supremely confident in their bodies, are wont to do. Only the behemoth linemen, with their pink, muffin-top bellies and flat asses, bothered to wrap a towel around their junk, which relative to their massive bodies always looked undersized. Morrison and his crew were grinding their pelvises to some rap song like stiff-limbed, Caucasian male strippers. Coaches walked through and merely shook their heads at the locker room shenanigans, which hadn't really changed much since they hung up their own jocks.

With my mind already wandering aimlessly in an uncertain future, I nostalgically soaked up the testosterone-inspired theater of the male adolescent absurd.

Chapter Fourteen

Thursday Night, November 1, 201_

Scags dropped me off in my driveway behind my dad's truck. With my head pounding a jackhammer's symphony, I just wanted to eat something and cocoon myself inside my room.

All of the lights were off inside the house except for the bluish glow of the television. I wasn't sure what it was, but something struck me as off. I'd come home to that same scene hundreds of times. But the second I entered the backdoor, I knew something was different. Something bad had happened.

"Mom?" I called. "Dad?"

The only response I received was my dad's panic snore, which happened whenever he was startled by external stimuli while lost inside a deep sleep.

I walked through the kitchen, where I passed my dad's new work shirt draped over a chair. I found him on the couch in the living room with his belt undone and his blue work pants unbuttoned and unzipped. He had returned to his default position passed out on the couch in front of the television. His feet were splayed out in front of him. His mouth was wide open, and his arm was extended over the arm of the couch with a beer bottle magically suspended in his hand.

"Dad?" I said, but received no response. "Dad?" I said louder with the same result.

I walked over and peeled his fingers from around the beer bottle, which, as I knew it would, set off alarm bells in his head.

"Hey! Give me that back," he said and grabbed the half-empty bottle from my hand. "Get your own beer."

"Dad, where's mom?"

"How the hell would I know? She's probably laying down. She said she had a headache."

Before I'd reached my parents' bedroom door, my dad's snore had resumed. I turned the glass doorknob and inched the door open wide enough to sneak my head inside and to cast a swath of light on their too small, full-sized mattress, where my mom lay flat on her back with a wet wash cloth draped across her forehead.

"Mom?" I whispered gently.

"T.J., honey. Is that you?"

"Yeah, Mom. Dad said you didn't feel well."

"It's just a headache, dear, but I can't seem to find my medicine. You know, the pills I'd given you for your headache. I keep them in the cabinet. I don't suppose you've seen the bottle?"

I avoided the subject by responding with a question of my own. "Should dad be drinking? He has to get up early for work."

My mom turned her head so that she faced away from me.

"Mom?"

"Your dad lost his job."

"What?" I asked; although, I'd heard her clearly.

She turned to face me and sat up against the brass rails of the headboard. "Your dad lost his job," she repeated.

"He what? What'd he do? Was he drinking?"

"No. He didn't do anything."

"He must have," I insisted. "That's not right. That can't be right. He just started. I'll talk to Doctor Stone. He'll know what to do. He'll call somebody and make it right."

"He's the one who called."

"Who? Who called?"

"Earlier. Caly's father. Dr. Stone called to apologize and to tell your father that there'd been some kind of budgetary error and the job was no longer available."

I lost it.

"That can't be. He promised. He can't FUCK with me like this!"

"T.J.!" My mom was shocked and offended by my language and anger.

"You don't understand, Mom. I know things. He owes me. He owes dad that job." My head throbbed and mocked my anger. I bent at the waist and pressed my palms into my temples. "Go . . . Away!" I screamed at the pain.

"T.J.!" She repeated. "What's the matter with you? You're talking crazy. It'll be okay. We'll get by; we always have."

"I'm tired of getting by. I had it all worked out. There was a plan, and now . . . and now it's . . . it's . . . . This doesn't make sense." I paced back and forth at the foot of the bed. "This . . . this isn't right."

"T.J.?"

"No! They're all in on it together."

"T.J.? Who's in on what?"

"Dr. Stone, Coach Harris, Coach Markinson, Chief Johnson. They're all out to get me – to ruin everything."

"T.J." She said once more, climbed out of the bed, and approached me gingerly from the side, as if I'd taken my own self hostage and had a gun pointed at my head. "I don't understand what you're saying. I don't know why you think all of those men are 'out to get you.'"

I ground the heels of my hands into my eyeballs in an attempt to dim the strobes that had commenced flashing incessantly inside my skull.

"Maybe," my Mom said, "you should go lay down. Get some rest." Gently, she placed one hand on my shoulder and the other in the small of my back.

I turned to her. "Oh, Mom," I said and collapsed into her arms and into a puddle of flesh and bone on the floor. She followed me down and held my head against her breasts and whispered, "It's okay, sweetheart. It's okay."

"I'm not going to get to play tomorrow. I won't get the scholarship. Caly broke up with me. And now Dad lost his job." I summarized the day through blubbering and running snot and tears. "I'm sorry, Mom. I'm so sorry."

"It's okay. It's going to be okay," she continued to repeat having little understanding of the list of personal tragedies that I was talking about. I suppose she believed that if she said it was going to be okay enough times, it may actually be true.

I wept on the cold hardwood floor for I don't know how long before my mom helped pick me up to my feet and led me to my room, where I crashed headlong onto my mattress.

*****

I'd been fading in and out of a fitful sleep when my phone sounded a muffled and unfamiliar ringtone from inside my pants pocket.

Bo, who at some point had joined me in my room, growled ominously at the interruption in his sleep.

"Quiet, boy," I said.

I didn't recognize the number but felt oddly compelled to answer. "Hello," I said. In the near pitch blackness, my voice sounded disembodied from its source.

"How's the headache?" A girl's voice asked.

"Who is this?" I sat up in bed a little too quickly and sent my black world spinning. "Perdita?"

"I can make it all go away."

"I need my pills."

"That's one way."

"What do you mean?"

125

"Meet me outside," she said and disconnected her cell.
The alarm clock showed 12:01 a.m.

Chapter Fifteen

Friday, Early Morning, All Souls Day, November 2, 201_

Still wearing my ripening thrift store clothes from what was, technically, two days earlier, I added my letter jacket as I passed through the mud room and exited the back door. At the intersection of Hill Road and Route 6, which was viewable from the small back porch, a pair of taillights flared and illuminated what looked to be the rear end and extra-wide wheel base of a classic Buick sport wagon, much like the one Mr. Mortis drove and Perdita and I had "borrowed." I found her leaning against the bed of the Ranger. She was dressed in her usual all black, including the black skull cap.

"You got keys for this piece of shit?" She asked.

"I need my pills."

"I need a ride."

"How'd you know where I lived?"

"I asked around. It didn't take long to find out. Apparently, you're some kind of football hero. Everyone in this town knows where you live."

"So what do you want? You stole my pills."

"*I* stole them? That's funny. Loretta Farrell?" She held the bottle up with the label turned towards me.

"Okay. They're my mom's, but I need them."

"And *I* told *you* that I need a ride."

"How'd you get here?"

"I thumbed it."

"Hitchhiked? What is this 1970?"

"Whatever."

"Why didn't your ride just take you to wherever it is you're going?"

"Because he dropped me off and got right back on the highway. I was hitchhiking. It wasn't a taxi service. And, because I'm not sure where I'm going. I need you to help me find the place."

"He?" I asked.

"What?"

"You said, 'he' dropped you off."

"Yeah. 'He.' Some guy. So what? Who cares?"

"Was that you?"

"Was what me?"

"At the party?"

"I go to a lot of parties."

"At the winery, where the kid got stabbed?"

Perdita hesitated. "You want the pills or do you want to play twenty questions?"

I didn't answer. It didn't really matter. Instead, I walked to the barn, went inside, and took the spare set of keys from the top drawer of my dad's dust-covered tool bench. "You're going to have to help me push it out. The engine is really loud, and I don't want to wake my parents. There's no way my mom would allow this. Push from the front." I shifted the truck into neutral and pushed from the driver's side door while occasionally steering with my left hand. "Hop in," I said when we reached the road. "Where we going?" I asked once she'd joined me in the cab.

"A party."

"A party? Now?"

Perdita looked at me like I was the most lame teenager in America.

"Okay. Where is it?"

"It's around here somewhere. This is Crystal Ridge, right?"

"Yeah."

"Do you know," she looked at a slip of paper she held in her hand, "some guy named Dalton?"

"Dalton isn't the first name; it's the family's name. There are a bunch of them."

"I'm sure we'll figure it out. Let's go."

"Can I have my pills?"

"Get me to the party and I'll give you the pills. Be good and you might get something extra."

I turned the key in the ignition, fired up the truck, put it into gear, and headed due north on Hill Road deep into Crystal Ridge to where in an eddy, created by the curved confluence of Hill and Bayshore roads, sat the Dalton family compound, an unwelcoming collection of fishing shacks, cottages, and outbuildings they called home and surrounded with "No Trespassing" signs. Over the years, they'd been approached many times with generous offers by developers who cherished the waterfront property, but each one had been rudely turned away – sometimes at the killing end of a shotgun – and few, if any, of those prospective buyers, possessed the necessary balls or greed required to make a second run at the Daltons.

Although it sat barely more than a mile from my home, I could count on one hand the number of times, including the recent Halloween excursion, that I'd even driven past the Dalton compound. Besides its being on the way to nowhere, as long as I could remember, my mom had made that section of Crystal Ridge off-limits and filled my head with such horrific stories of the Dalton clan that I obeyed her restriction wholeheartedly. For the nine years during which I rode the bus to school, I'd been forbidden to sit next to or even to talk with the Dalton children, of which there were many. Their school attendance was occasional at best, especially during the picking season when many of them worked the fields side-by-side with the migrant laborers. More than a few of such migrants had achieved their golden ticket to America by marrying into the Dalton brood, which only furthered local antipathy and created a strange blend of Anglo-Mexican cross-breeding so that many of the Dalton clan were actually named Garcia, Marquez, or Araguz. During the spring walleye run or the late summer perch season, when bait fish were in high demand and many hands were required for sorting, the Dalton kids were almost never in school. For their part, the Dalton offspring showed about as much interest in assimilating into the Goodness Falls school community as their parents showed in being part of Goodness Falls at large, which is to say they showed no interest at all. Remarkably, a fairly amicable co-existence had been maintained for at least four or five generations between villagers and the Daltons based on a mutual mistrust, a healthy dislike, and staying the hell out of each others' way.

The pain in my head was so bad, however, that I didn't care about my mother's warnings or the pariah status of the Daltons. I only knew that I desperately needed the Vicodin, and I was willing to go damn near anywhere to get it back. Once I dropped Perdita off at her party, I planned to return home, swallow a few pills, and get a decent sleep for what was left of the evening.

"What kind of party is this?" I asked Perdita.

"The best kind of party," she answered cryptically. "It's a celebration. A homecoming."

She clearly had little interest in telling me more, so I drove on in silence. What did I care anyway? I only wanted my pills.

In a matter of minutes, we drew near to the Daltons' place. Adjacent to the rear of the property, separated by only a foreboding black wrought iron fence, lay the Crystal Ridge cemetery, which was illuminated a hellish red by roadside flares spaced throughout the grounds and spewing liquid fire. Fireworks intermittently arced towards the sky, exploded, and rained down in streams of white light towards the ghoulish figures milling about below. Sparklers in the hands of children etched zigzag patterns in the darkness among the tombstones. It looked like a ghoulish Independence Day celebration.

At the front of the property, torches lined and lit the lanes that entered the compound from both Hill and Bayshore roads and formed a horseshoe drive. A little freaked and confused by the macabre graveyard celebration, I stopped the truck on the road. "There you go," I said. "Can I have my pills now?"

"No," Perdita said. "I said you have to take me to the party, not drop me off on the road."

I didn't like the idea one bit, but I was desperate enough to go along. I pulled into the lane from Hill Road. Interspersed between the torches were what looked like human skulls on crossed sticks raised like scarecrows. Most wore hats of various sorts and each of the sticks was draped in men's or women's clothing. There were even a few shorter sticks with children's skulls and clothes.

"What is this?" I asked, as I came to a stop in front of one of the homes. Its windows were framed in multi-colored Christmas lights.

"I told you. It's a celebration. It's Dia de las muertos." She announced in her state of absolute enthrallment.

"What?"

"The festival of the dead. November 2ⁿᵈ. The 'day' of the dead literally, but for many, especially Mexicans, it's a celebration of All Saints and All Souls Day combined. They believe that on this day dead friends and relatives can be enticed home to hear prayers and to communicate with the living."

"This is too weird," I said. "Give me the pills. I want to get out of here." But in the next second, the way forward was blocked by a mob of Daltons. Many wore what looked like Mexican wrestling masks. Others had their faces painted white with black circles around the eyes and lips to look like exposed skulls.

"What's up with all of the skulls?"

"They honor the dead," she answered just as a pickup full of the Daltons we'd passed in the graveyard pulled in behind me and blocked my path of retreat. In the bed of the truck stood another of the skull-headed scarecrows. However, its near seven-foot height, elaborate costume, and the veneration it received upon its arrival made clear its greater significance than those that lined the lane. It was a full skeleton dressed in black robes. In one hand, it held a scythe, in the other a globe. "What is that?" I asked Perdita.

"Who is that?" She corrected me.

"*Who* is that then?"

"La Santa Muerte. Saint Death."

"Can I *please* have my pills?" I whined, totally weirded out.

"No. Come and get them," Perdita said and climbed from the truck into a chorus of enthusiastic greetings and embracing arms. The Dalton clan swarmed to her and washed her into the house, leaving me alone inside the truck. A half hour earlier, she supposedly had no idea who the Daltons were or how to even find the place. Something wasn't right, but made desperate and reckless by the pain, I got out and followed her inside.

The interior was a train wreck pastiche of all things redneck or Mexican. In its origins, the home had been a rustic fishing cabin with an open floor plan. A counter/eating space separated the Spartan kitchen from the living area with a small bathroom attached to the rear of the kitchen. The upstairs was an open loft lined with bunk beds. Dark eyes of curious children peered down in between the spindles of the wooden railing at the edge of the loft. The couches and chairs had all been pushed to the periphery to form a dancing space in the center of the tiled first floor, where La Sante Muerte was brought inside and stationed as a sort of maypole around which worshippers danced. Tejano music spilled from an old-school turntable connected with wires to wooden speakers hung from the wall. The dancing was a mixture of country line dancing and zapateado which left an abundance of heel marks on the floor. The Stars and Bars of the Confederacy shared wall space with a flag of Mexico and those of several NASCAR and Mexican League soccer teams. A variety of crucifixes populated the walls, and portraits of Mary hung in ornate and gilded frames.

A makeshift altar of foldable tables, draped with multi-colored and blinking Christmas lights, lined the entire length of one wall. Incense burners and lit candles of every color, size, and scent covered its top and burned on the floor dangerously close to the altar cloths. Flowers bloomed everywhere on and around the altar. A sumptuous buffet of tamales, bread, doughnut-shaped rolls pierced by sugar sticks, barbecued pork, cornbread, salt shakers, and bottled water was on the altar – not for the living guests but for the deceased ancestors who'd be traveling that night. Photographs of dead relatives tenanted the space as well. Also on the altar, friends and family had placed a flea market-worthy number of personal items special to their deceased loved ones. Bars of soap were also provided with which the deceased sojourners could refresh themselves upon arrival.

From my wallet, I removed a school photograph of Moose that I'd been carrying since freshman year and set it on the altar. I then used the key to the pickup to pluck at the threads that held my varsity "GF" letter to my letterman's jacket until I could tear it off completely. I placed it next to the photo.

I turned and scanned the room for Perdita, who emerged as if on cue from the boot-scooting and twirling dancers. She held up two closed fists out in front of her like some old-fashioned, bare-knuckled boxer.

"You can have these," she rattled the Vicodin inside the plastic bottle in her left hand, "go home, go to sleep, and wake up with your head still hurting in your boring little white bread world, or you can have these." She rattled the pill bottle in her right hand, which was full of multi-colored pills that looked like tiny SweeTart candies. "Mollies," she explained. "They're killer. You'll swallow a few, forget about your problems, have some fun with Perdita, and all of the pain will be gone for good."

My eyes relayed back and forth from one of Perdita's hands to the other.

"The choice is yours," she said.

I knew what I *should* do. There was no moral confusion. However, In the previous twelve hours, I'd watched my world and my future collapse around me. I was in pain. I was weak. And I had little left to lose. "What are mollies?" I asked, pointing at the candy-colored pills.

"E, baby. Ecstasy. It's all E. Extra strength and home grown right here in the Dalton family laboratory."

"What will they do?"

"They'll make you a god."

I extended my hand towards her and split the difference between the two pill bottles. My hand hung suspended and uncommitted for a few moments before I tapped her right hand. "What the fuck?"

Perdita smiled widely. "That's right. What the fuck? Open wide."

I parted my lips. Perdita poured a molly from the bottle then, with the pill squeezed between her thumb and middle finger, she ran her index finger slowly around my lips and teased me before setting it on my tongue like a communion wafer. I closed my lips over her finger as if it were a nipple. She slowly extracted her finger, replaced it with her wintry lips, then inserted her tongue into my mouth as if to verify that I had swallowed the pill.

At first, the ecstasy had little effect, but within a half hour, I began to feel more alive than at any previous point in my sorry excuse for a life. My heart beat at an accelerated rate. The colors of the Christmas lights were sharper. The notes in the songs clearer. Perdita served me shots of tequila that burned my throat. I was pretty sure I saw one of the Chicano Dalton men eating a skull from off the altar. New arrivals, costumed as ghosts, zombies, and skeletons, arrived intermittently throughout the night. Most importantly, as Perdita promised, the pain went away. When I danced with her, electric currents passed between us, and when we kissed, I tasted the afterlife. She was right. I *was* a god.

Hours passed like seconds. At one point, while awkwardly faking my way through some dance with Perdita, Mr. Mortis walked past us in super slow motion and gave her an approving nod.

Dia de la muertes, I thought. *Dia de la Mortis.*

Around four a.m., Perdita took me by the hand and led me outside. We climbed into the pickup. She reached inside her top and bra and removed the bottle of Vicodin. She poured a handful into her palm, closed the lid, then slid the bottle into my jeans pocket, where she allowed her fingers to linger teasingly on the inside of my thigh.

"Open up," she said. "But chew them this time before swallowing. You'll be glad you did."

I opened my mouth. Perdita placed several tablets on her tongue one at a time then transferred them to mine with a deep kiss. I chewed each one and swallowed.

The comedown effects were nearly immediate. I could feel my heart slowing down and the blood returning to my core. In a moment of epiphanic clarity between the high from the ecstasy and the crash from the Vicodin, I looked deeply into Perdita's black eyes. "Are you trying to kill me, Perdita?"

"The pain is almost over," she said and kissed me once more, deeply and long. She ran her bony fingers through my hair, then lightly traced my ears and inspired layers of gooseflesh to surface all over my body. She held an index finger in front of my face. The tip was dabbed with blood from my ear. She whispered, "Golden lads and girls all must, as chimney sweepers, come to dust."

"I suppose that's Shakespeare."

"That's right, baby. Night, night."

*****

At some point – I'm not sure what time it was – I woke up, or maybe not, maybe I dreamt it or, as Dr. Young insists, I just hallucinated it. Anyway, instead of Perdita, it was Mr. Mortis who sat on the passenger's side of the pickup.

"Mr. Mortis," I said. "What are you doing here?"

"The better question, T.J., is what are *you*, still doing here. Perdita fed you a cocktail that should have put down a newbie like you an hour ago."

"So she really was trying to kill me," I said more to myself than to him.

"But," he ignored my accusation, "to answer your original question, I'm waiting for you."

"Waiting for me to do what?" I asked.

"To die, T.J. What else? Haven't you been paying attention this past week?"

"I'm sorry?" I said, meaning that I wasn't sure I'd heard him correctly, but Mr. Mortis took it differently.

"No need to be sorry. Most people share your reluctance but not your talent for avoiding the inevitable.

"Wait. You're being serious aren't you?"

"Dead serious. Think about it: a vicious blow to the head, a tractor trailer with your name on it, several more brutal head shots at practice, a near-miss stabbing, and now a lethal mixture of drugs and alcohol assault on your nearly virginal system. Just be glad you never did go duck hunting. That would have been messy."

"So you're like the Grim Reaper?"

"I'm not 'like' anything, T.J. I am what I am. But that's one of the names people use."

"You're Death?" I asked incredulously.

"Not exactly. Death is a condition, a nothingness. It's not a being. I'm more like a collector."

"You mean like a guide to the next world?"

"No. I think I told you once before, there is no next world."

"I can't believe you came here just for me."

"Don't flatter yourself. I haven't. There have been others. Do I need to list them?"

"No," I said in a despondent tone.

"Believe it or not, I don't always control or even exactly know the how, when, or order of deaths. Sometimes, I'm surprised myself."

"You just show up for work?"

"You might say that."

"Have you ever been wrong or have you ever changed your mind?"

"Not yet."

"Why me?"

"That's a silly question. Why not you?"

"That's a silly answer."

"It's all I've got."

"But people aren't just dying in Goodness Falls," I said. "They have to be dying all over the world."

"That's correct, and they are. Ubiquitous, remember? I'm always around, T.J. I'm around so often and in so many different forms that few people notice me. I'm the substitute teacher, the bus driver, the delivery guy, the emergency room nurse, the virus on the doorknob, the unexplained lump in the nut sack."

"What about heaven and hell?"

"Nonsense."

"Really?" I asked disappointedly.

"Really."

"Will I see a light or something?"

"You might – for a while. Trust me. It'll be fine. It looks quite nice, death. I actually envy you." He assumed a faraway gaze that I recognized from his recitations in class.

"Oh, no," I said. "Not again. You're not going to . . ."

"To die – too sleep: no more; . . ."

"Quote Shakespeare," I finished too late.

". . . and by a sleep to say we end the heart-ache and the thousand natural shocks that flesh is heir to, tis a consummation devoutly to be wished.' *Hamlet*."

"What's with all the Shakespeare?" I asked.

"In all the history of mankind, he's the only one I regretted collecting. He's the only one who came close to understanding."

"Understanding what?"

"Everything."

"What about Perdita?"

"She works for me."

"What is she?"

"Dead."

"I thought you said . . ."

"She's the exception."

"I'm afraid."

"Don't be. Nothing is nothing to be afraid of."

"I guess not."

"I really must be going. I don't want to be late for class." He opened the door, which illuminated the cab of the truck. "T.J., it's been a pleasure. I will say I do enjoy the occasional challenge."

I tried to prolong his stay, but I was already alone and on the verge of release.

Chapter Sixteen

Friday Morning, All Souls Day, November 2, 201_

In all truth, I didn't want to come back. I'd thought I'd already escaped. The pain had gone away; the dark was soundless and deep, like I imagine space. Even though my skin felt cold and clammy, a warm serenity infused my insides. My heart beat at a nearly imperceptible rate, and I felt as if I were as light as air.

"Hey, buddy. Hey, T-Bag."

"Oh, Christ," I complained. "Now who? Moose? Is that you?" I asked and struggled to lift my head just enough off of the cold vinyl of the seat – to which my drool had all but plastered my cheek – to see Moose's thick legs.

"It's time to wake up. Time to rally. You can't stay here any longer," he said between bites of a tamale.

"But I like it here," I whined like a five-year-old, lowered my face to the seat, and began to slide back into the coma-like sleep. "Besides, Dr. Stone, Caly, even Mr. Mortis say you don't exist. You're a hallucination."

"Hey, douche bag!" Moose said loudly. "Get your ass up. This is your two-minute warning. It's now or never. *Carpe Diem*, motherfucker."

At my core, I felt something unwanted rising to the surface and dragging my consciousness with it. I opened my eyes and gasped. Natural light seared my retinas and cold morning air burned my lungs. My insides were in revolt. I lifted my head and army crawled towards the passenger side door. I grasped for the handle, nudged the door open, and vomited, which – I've been told – is what saved my life.

When I sat up, I didn't even bother looking for Moose. I knew he wouldn't be there. But on the dash sat my varsity "GF" and Moose's photograph. I glanced at my ghoulish reflection in the rear view mirror. Pale skin stretched tautly over my increasingly-bearded cheekbones. Jaundiced eyes stared back at me from dark and hollowed out sockets. A slow rotation of my head revealed a thin trickle of dried blood along my upper jaw line emanating from my ear. Ghostlike memories of the festival of the dead flitted around inside my head. "Perdita," I said. But she wasn't there either.

I found the pill bottle inside my jeans pocket where Perdita had left it; however, it was empty. Either she had stolen what was left or I had consumed them. I really didn't know which was the truth. I dropped it onto the seat.

I stumbled out of the truck and squinted against the harsh daylight. Spinning slowly on my heels, I turned a full circle and surveyed the compound. The torches and skeleton scarecrows were gone. Spasms of excruciating pain returned, ran circuits over and around my skull, and forced me to lean against the truck to avoid falling to the ground.

I made my way determinedly to the house, opened the unlocked door, and discovered it full of children: some at the counter eating cereal, others seated or lying in front of a television set, which replayed a soccer match on one of the Spanish language channels. There was no dance floor, no Christmas lights, no crucifixes, no altar.

"Perdita?" I asked.

The children looked at me momentarily.

"The lost girl," a black haired, almond-eyed boy, sitting on his haunches in front of the television, confirmed Mrs. Martinez's translation. Then he and the other children returned to their breakfasts and to the soccer game without further reply.

After shutting the door, I returned to the pickup and tried to collect my thoughts. At first, I wasn't even sure what day of the week it was. Then it hit me: "Shit! It's Friday! What time is it?" I asked out loud to no one. "I need to get to school." I hurried around to the driver's side and climbed back inside of the truck. I found my cell on the dash. It read 8:52. I was already late. And my mom. What must she be thinking?

I sped up Hill Road while listening to the messages in my in-box on speakerphone. Every one of them was from my mom, beginning around six a.m. The panic in her voice increased exponentially with each message left in five to ten minute intervals. Each inquired of my whereabouts.

When I fishtailed to a stop in the driveway, Bo raced out of the back door ahead of my mom. At such homecomings, he would typically greet me by standing on his back legs, placing his forepaws against me, and licking at my face, but as he approached, he caught a whiff of something on me that stopped him dead in his tracks. He whimpered fearfully and lowered himself to the ground.

"It's okay, boy. I'm okay."

My mom waddled out of the back door still in her frumpy nightgown, robe, and bath slippers. "Where have you been?!" She screamed through her tears. "I called the hospital and the school. I even called the police. They're out looking for you."

I should have lied, said anything but the truth, but I answered, "The Daltons'."

"The Daltons'!" She echoed my confession. "Why? You know you're not supposed to go near those people."

"I don't know. I don't remember."

"Are you doing drugs?!"

"Mom, no."

"Then why were you at the Daltons? Are you doing drugs?" She asked again.

"Mom, I'm not doing drugs. I swear," I had to stop her line of questioning before she realized the accuracy of her accusation. "I'm going to take the truck and get to school. I need to be there before noon, or I can't even dress out for the game tonight. I'm going to make everything right. I promise."

"Honey, you look awful. I don't think you should go to school."

"I have to, Mom. I have to be at the game tonight." I leaned in and kissed her on the cheek. "I've got to go."

I jumped back inside the truck. I hadn't showered, shaved, or changed my clothes for two days. I hadn't even brushed my teeth and I didn't care. The empty pill bottle, which I'd left carelessly exposed on the seat, drew my attention. I picked it up and checked inside, hoping I had somehow missed one or that the Vicodin fairies had come. There was no way I could face the day with the hammer that was continuing to pound against my skull. Finding no pills inside, I bent over, plugged a nostril, and tried to snort what little dust lined the inside walls and bottom of the bottle. I even stuck my tongue inside as far as it would go then wet my pinkie, swabbed the plastic sides, and sucked off my finger. I was beyond pathetic. Defeated and on the verge of tossing the empty bottle onto the floor with the rest of the trash, the label on the front drew my attention. I read, "Refills: One."

Driven by desperation and renewed hope, I backed out and headed for Ben's Deep Discount Store up town. I wasn't sure who the "Ben" was named on the sign, but I knew the pharmacist was Miss Kennedy, a longtime Goodness Falls spinster and a huge Ducks fan. Other than the Get-Go, Ben's was the only store of any sort less than a fifteen-minute drive to one of the big box stores south of Sandusky. It was a favorite after school/after practice stop for candy, chips, and pop. If she wasn't in the back busy filling prescriptions, Miss Kennedy would come out and run a second register whenever the store was being overrun by school kids. She treated every kid like a customer, not as a potential shoplifter like the other workers did.

I parallel parked on Main Street directly in front of the store. Its windows, like the other downtown shops and businesses, were still painted in harvest and Halloween scenes as part of an expired contest among middle school classrooms. The business end of a bunch of half-priced, fan-styled leaf rakes stuck out of a big cardboard box. They battled for space and the attention of the more forward-thinking shoppers with a similar-sized box of plastic-bladed snow shovels. Pallets holding bags of rock salt and pallets of blue wiper fluid filled-in the remaining sidewalk space. Before entering, I caught my reflection in the storefront glass. It took me an extra second or two to realize that the face of the disheveled kid staring back at me *was* me. I tucked my t-shirt into my pants, zipped up my hoodie, buttoned up my letter jacket with a deep red "GF" and loose threads hanging where the varsity letter had been, and ran my fingers through my tousled hair, but there was nothing I could do to restore the person who had been T.J. Farrell to his place in that town, those clothes, and in that body.

A bell rang overhead when I entered. Each ting-a-ling reverberated painfully between my ears. A cashier, whom I didn't recognize, nodded her indifferent awareness of my presence from her station at the only open cash register, where she was busy placing drastically-reduced prices on a host of Halloween-themed items. I headed directly towards the pharmacy counter in the rear, where I could see Miss Kennedy in a white lab coat moving about among the rows of tall shelves of pills and powders and syrups and salves. She caught sight of my approach and smiled instinctively, but her expression almost immediately morphed into something other than "Hello." It asked, "Shouldn't you be in school?"

I distracted her from asking her question with one of my own. "Hey, Miss Kennedy. You coming to the game tomorrow night?"

"Of course I'm coming. What kind of question is that. Haven't missed one, home or away, in nearly thirty years. But what are you doing in here? Are you sick? You don't look so good." She reached over the counter and felt my cheek and forehead for fever with the back of her hand.

"I'm fine, Miss Kennedy," I said and set the empty pill bottle on the counter, "but my mom is . . . um . . . she's . . . um . . . having some pain. She had a root canal, I think, not too long ago that, I guess, is hurting her pretty bad."

She picked up the bottle and studied the label. "That was nearly three months ago," she said.

"I don't know. She just asked me to get this prescription refilled. She said that you know her and would help her out." I took a chance and added, "If you want, I can call her on my cell and you can talk to her yourself." I bluffed and pulled my phone out of my jacket pocket.

"No, honey. Don't bother the poor thing if she's not feeling well." She read the label again then took a long look into my eyes. "This is Vicodin, T.J. It's a pretty strong medicine."

"Is it?" I asked with as much innocence as I could muster.

She read the label out loud. I think more for her benefit than mine. "One refill," she said. I could almost hear her thinking, *It's just one refill.*

"It's not a problem, Miss Kennedy. I can go somewhere else. It's just that it says 'Ben's' on the label and I was hoping to get these pills back to my mom so that I can get to school. I'm already late."

"No, no. I'll fill it. You wait here," she said and disappeared among the shelves for a few minutes.

Over the counter next to the cash register, I noticed a little white bag stapled shut and with an enlarged pill bottle label with dosage instructions stuck on the front. I looked over my shoulder toward the front of the store. The cashier was nowhere in sight and the aisles were empty of customers. I leaned over the counter so that I could see Miss Kennedy through the open shelves with her back turned and filling my mom's prescription. As slyly and quietly as possible, I reached over and turned the white bag so that the label was readable. One word jumped off the label and from out of my memory of Perdita's initial disappointed reaction to my Vicodin: Percocet. As quietly as possible and with my eyes trained on Miss Kennedy the entire time, I gently lifted the bag, pulled it over the counter, and stuffed it inside the pouch on my hoodie inside of my letter jacket.

"Here you go, T.J." Miss Kennedy called as she returned to the counter. "There are twenty pills here," she said as she slipped the bottle into a white bag like the one I'd stolen. "That'll be $17.99."

I hadn't thought about how I'd pay for the pills. "I don't know if I have that much money. I was in a hurry and forgot to get some from my mom." From my wallet and pockets, I managed to dump a little more than thirteen bucks in bills and change on the counter. "That's all I have."

"Oh, honey. I'd help you out but it's store policy."

"I wouldn't ask, but it's just that my mom really seemed to be in a lot of pain."

"Hold on," Miss Kennedy said. She walked to the back of the pharmacy. I watched her remove a billfold from her purse and extract some cash. "Now, don't you tell anyone. I could get in a lot of trouble. I'll loan you the five. You tell your mother she can pay me back the next time she's in the store."

"That's great," I said. "I'll do that. Thanks so much, Miss Kennedy."

"You just go out and beat Lakeview tonight."

"I will or we will," I said.

"And T.J.," she added. "Before you go to school, why don't you clean up a little. You want to make a good impression on that cheerleader girlfriend of yours don't you?"

Her reference to Caly damn near took the wind out of me. I struggled for a few seconds to answer. "Yes, M'am. I do. And I will," I said and backed away from the counter. "Have a good day, Miss Kennedy." I waved goodbye, then turned around and all but ran from the store.

I didn't even bother to turn on the engine before I removed the bag containing the Percocet from my hoodie, tore it open, threw it among all of the other trash on the floor, and poured one, then two, then three pills from the bottle. Amongst the trash on the floor, I found one Gatorade bottle with enough drink and backwash still in the bottom to help me choke the pills down.

I had just leaned my head against the back window of the cab and begun waiting for the warmth to rekindle and the pain to go away, when I heard a tapping on the driver's side window no more than six inches from my ear. It startled the shit out of me.

I cranked down the window. "Hey, Chief."

"T.J. Farrell. We've been over half the county looking for you."

"I'm sorry about all of that, Chief. My mom and I had a misunderstanding that's all. I was out scouting some new duck blind locations over in Bay View. You've got to do that early in the morning. I told her, but she must have forgotten where I was. I lost track of the time, and now I'm late for school. That's all. It's all good now."

"Well, you're right about getting er done early. Does your mother know where you are now?"

"Yes, sir. She does. Actually, she sent me into town to fill her prescription before I go to school."

"Is that right?"

I could see his eyes move with suspicion to the prescription bag sitting on the seat next to me."

"Do you mind if I take a look?" He pointed to the bag.

I knew he had no legal right to do so, and I could have refused. But I was afraid that would only raise his already elevated suspicions regarding my recent behaviors and most likely extend the conversation that was fast-becoming uncomfortable. Thankful that I had chosen to open the Percocet instead of the Vicodin, I handed him the still-stapled and closed bag with my mom's name on it.

While he read the usage label on front, out of the corner of my eye, I noticed the empty white bag that had contained the Percocet prescription lying conspicuously amongst the trash on the floor, and I felt the bottle of pills buzzing on the seat where I had squeezed it between my legs. I was fairly sure he wouldn't notice the bag, but if he asked me to get out of the truck for any reason I was screwed.

"Vicodin," he said. "That's a pretty powerful pill. Twenty of these would fetch you a good chunk of pocket change around here."

"Really?" I said, playing dumb.

"Really. I want you to look into my eyes, son." He held up a finger and said, "Follow my finger with your eyes. Just your eyes." He moved his finger back and forth while he stared into my eyes for what seemed forever. "Do you realize that your left pupil is about twice the size of your right one?"

"No, sir."

"Of course, you don't." Apparently, however, his curiosity was satisfied with what he saw. "Okay, T.J. You be good to your mama, get your butt into school, and keep your head up tonight."

"No need to worry about that, Chief. I've been benched."

"That's right. I read that in the paper. By the way, Coach confirmed your story about the Cabriolet. I'm closing the Mooseburger case. I guess the truth won't out after all. It's really a shame."

As the Percocet continued to pump its mellow magic through my veins, all was immediately better, if not yet right, inside my head and with my world. I was quickly losing interest or concern for the Chief's musings. I simply nodded my head in agreement to whatever it was he was saying. "I got to go, Chief."

He tapped the roof of the pickup. "You're right. Get out of here. And good luck tonight, even if you're not playing. Go Ducks."

Chapter Seventeen

Friday Mid-Morning, All Souls Day, November 2, 201_

After the first bell, the only way of ingress into the school building was through the main entrance beneath the suspicious eye of a camera and the even more suspicious eyes of the secretary in the attendance office, who, either upon recognizing the student or asking the visitor to state his or her business, would buzz him in.

I approached with my hands deep in my pockets and my head beneath my hood, so I heard him before I saw him.

"I'll be damned," he said in a tone of genuine surprise but completely free of irony, anger, or disappointment.

"Mr. Mortis," I said by way of greeting. "I bet you didn't expect to see me today."

"I did not. Your name was on the absence list this morning, and there's talk all over school of your melt downs this week with Coach Harris, Caly, Pete Terwilliger. Should I go on?"

"No."

"There are even rumors of you drinking, smoking pot, and taking pills. Say it ain't so," he said through a knowing smirk.

"Yeah? Well, it's a small town. People talk," I dodged the truthful accusations. "But what about you? Where are you going?"

"Until now, I was under the impression that my services were no longer required in Goodness Falls, especially when Mr. Miller showed up for class today. You know, 'Life goes on' and all that, I suppose. But, here you are."

"Here I am. What will you do now?" I asked.

"Oh, I won't be too far. I have my hand in a number of things. I'm sure you'll see me again. Ubiquitous, remember?"

"That's right."

"You take care, T.J. It's been a rare pleasure," Mr. Mortis said and walked away.

"Mr. Mortis!" I called and stopped his progress. "What about Perdita?"

I'd no more than finished saying her name than the Buick Sport Wagon pulled up in front of the school with Perdita behind the wheel. Mr. Mortis turned towards me. "Death, too, goes on," he said and continued towards the car.

I thought for a minute and tried to separate the week's partially-remembered fragments of words and events – lived or imagined – into their appropriate categories of dreams, visions, drug-induced hallucinations, or reality. But I failed. The inside of my head was a wet mishmash of scrambled eggs. "Wait!" I called again to Mr. Mortis. "Are you real? Are you really . . ."

My question was cut short by the closing of the Buick Sport Wagon's heavy steel door.

I signed in a little before ten o'clock. My ragged appearance inspired the same muted look of disgust from the attendance office secretary as it had inspired in both my mom and Miss Kennedy. As much as I wanted just to lie down in a Percocet haze and as much as I dreaded the idea of sitting through my classes, I'd already laid my nurse card and had no others to play. There was little choice other than to suffer through my normal schedule, but with less than half the time left in third period, I decided to wait it out in the library and to report to fourth period at the change of classes.

For better or worse, I found Caly sitting alone and in front of one of the computers arranged in a circular island around a center utilities pole. The Percocet was reaching its peak performance period. I had achieved as much lucidity as I could expect before the pendulum would swing back in favor of the pain, so I determined to confront her. I had nothing left to lose: no girlfriend, no playing time, no scholarship, no future.

She didn't see me approach. "Hey," I said.

"Hey," she answered and continued to type.

"What you working on?"

"An early admissions essay." She wasn't going to make it easy.

"Can we talk?"

"Free country," she said dismissively, "but I've got to get this finished, and the bell's going to ring."

"We've got nearly twenty minutes. I only need ten. Then I promise, I'll leave you alone."

Caly stopped typing and rested her hands on her lap, but she refused to look at me.

"I'm sorry," was my predictable and weak gambit.

She rolled her eyes and sighed.

"I didn't want or plan for any of this to happen."

"But you've ruined everything!" Caly couldn't hold it in. She spoke a little too loudly and was shushed by the volunteer mom playing at librarian. "You ruined everything," Caly repeated in a whisper.

"Can I at least explain?"

"Explain what? There's nothing to explain."

"Look," I said. "I'm not asking for us to get back together or for you to forgive me. I'm only asking to tell my side of things as best as I can. Then, you can believe me, call me crazy like everyone else, or tell me to go to Hell. I don't care. I just want my chance."

I interpreted her silence as reluctant acquiescence.

"The truth is that I took a pretty good hit to the head last week, and I haven't been myself since."

Caly snapped her face towards me. "I told you to see a doctor."

"I know, but I couldn't. You know my history. The doctor would have benched me for sure."

"Then you should have let him bench you."

"That's easy for you to say. With your dad arranging for the Toledo coach to come watch me play? I couldn't do that."

"So you didn't go to the doctor for me?" She said sarcastically.

"No. For us. I was thinking about us, but things got worse."

"Moose?"

"Yeah, Moose." I hesitated and weighed the value and potential additional damage of continuing but decided to tell the truth, at least as best as I could determine it. "Caly, we caused the accident. Your father did anyway."

"Really, T.J.? That's where this is going? Blaming my father after all he's tried to do for you?"

"It's the truth. I'm not saying he meant for it to happen, but he pulled out in front of Mr. Mooseburger's truck and caused him to swerve off the road." Caly's faraway eyes betrayed that my description of events rang true for her and that she was replaying what were probably countless similar incidents she'd experienced while driving with her father. I pressed on. "If Mr. Mooseburger hadn't swerved, I'd be dead. But your dad . . . he wouldn't stop. He blamed Mr. Mooseburger. Even after we learned that Moose was dead, your father insisted we don't tell anyone the truth. He said it would ruin everything for me, for you, and for both of our families. It made sense at the time, so I went along."

"I can't believe that . . ."

"Just listen. I told your father how it was eating me up inside and how badly I wanted to tell the truth, but he'd already gone and got my dad a job at his hospital and told me to keep my shit together and everything would be okay. But, I couldn't. I couldn't keep my shit together."

"Your head?"

"Yeah. That and the guilt. I got trashed at Tucker's party, damn near raped you, missed practice, got into a fight with Coach Harris, and got benched. Somewhere in there, I started seeing Moose's ghost. Then I started stealing my mom's pain medicine and hanging around with the wrong people."

"That new girl?"

"And others. But, Caly, it gets worse."

"Worse? How can it get worse? You've all but accused my father of murder."

"The Cabriolet."

"What about it?" She asked defensively.

"Your father made us lie about it. Your mother and me. He made us tell Chief Johnson that he and I drove to and from Toledo in it. But we all know that he didn't have that car on Saturday morning."

"My father loves cars. He goes through them like shoes. I can't keep track of all of his cars," she said, but I could tell she knew the truth.

"Caly, he told me that the Cabriolet belongs to a nurse friend of his from work. He has the title, but it's her car."

"So, now you're telling me that my father is cheating on my mother. Is this your way of justifying your cheating on me? Are you going to tell me that all guys do it, so it's no big deal?"

"I'm not suggesting anything. I'm just saying we lied to protect him and to protect you."

"Why are you telling me this?"

"Because he's turned on me. He's turned on us. He doesn't believe he can rely on me, so he's trying to destroy me in your eyes and everyone else's."

"Wow! Aren't you a little full of yourself? Can you say paranoid?"

"He has to make me seem like an unreliable witness, so that even if I would tell the truth, no one would believe me."

"You've done a good enough job of that yourself."

"I'm pretty sure that he's made some kind of deal with Coach Harris not to play me regardless so that I'll lose the scholarship. Coach already told me that your dad has recommended him for a job on Toledo's staff next year."

"So, let me get this straight. You're the innocent victim of a massive conspiracy among, let me see, my father, my mother, Coach Harris, the University of Toledo, and, oh yeah, Moose's ghost, all to break us up and to make you appear insane so that your testimony would be worthless in court."

"I know it sounds crazy."

"Not 'sounds' crazy, T.J. It *is* crazy."

"And I haven't even told you about Mr. Mortis and Perdita yet."

"Mr. Mortis? What does Mr. Mortis and your little chica have to do with any of this?"

"I'm pretty sure they were trying to kill me."

I'd never before seen a look of disgust to match the one she gave me. The bell rang to end third period.

"I've got to go," Caly said. She shut down the computer, gathered her things, and rose to leave.

I grabbed her arm, probably a little too tightly. "Just think about it," I begged her. "Please. I've been a little mixed up in the head, but I'm not crazy. Here, take these. Throw them away," I said and handed her the bottle of Percocet. "I want to get my head straight. I'm going to go to a doctor. I promise. After the game."

Caly hesitated but took the pill bottle and stuffed it inside of her purse. "I've got to go, " she repeated, turned, and began to walk away.

"Always?" I pathetically tried once more .

She stopped. I watched her shoulders rise and fall as she took in a deep breath before she continued on her way out of the library without turning around or saying another word.

Chapter Eighteen

Friday Afternoon, All Souls Day, November 2, 201_

The remainder of the school day was torture. The pain began kicking the Percocet's ass. By noon I hated myself for giving the bottle over to Caly and leaving the Vicodin in the truck. Oddly enough, I was disappointed by Mr. Mortis's absence from English class. Mr. Miller was clearly still in mild shock over his wife's passing and not ready for the return to the classroom. He assigned us some independent reading and worksheets and stared out his window at a gorgeous oak to whose branches its orange and yellow leaves clung desperately.

As was tradition, after school the boosters hosted a game day dinner for the football players and cheerleaders at the VFW hall. There was more pasta and bread consumed in one of these carbohydrate binges than the entire independent nation of San Marino could eat in a month. The incessant din of nervous and excited teenage voices pushed my pain needle well into the red, which left me in no mood for food or conversation. In fact, it took all of my resolve to talk myself out of running to the pickup and tearing open the bag with the Vicodin inside. But I had promised Caly and myself that I was through with the pills, and I was determined to keep that promise. After the game, my plan was to have my mom drive me to the emergency room, where I'd relent to a full examination and cop to my abuse of the pain meds.

I sat alone with my back to the others at a table in a dark corner of the hall that had been my and Moose's lucky table all season. Absentmindedly, I pushed my spaghetti around on my plate and thought of better days. My teammates and the coaches had ignored, even avoided, me ever since I'd arrived. It was as if *I* had died, and I was already a ghost. In a way, I guess I had and I was. That line of wishful thinking was quickly snuffed out, however, when Moose joined me at our table.

"Are you all right, man?" He asked.

"Yeah," I lied, no longer surprised or frightened by his appearances. "You really ought to do something about that head wound."

"I think it makes me look tough. Besides, look who's talking. Yours has you talking to dead people."

"Good point. Seriously," I said, "why are you hanging around?"

"It's game day."

"No, I mean why are you still *here*?"

"There's no place else to go."

"What's it like?"

"Being dead?"

"Yeah."

"Dull. Just plain dull."

"That sucks," I said.

Moose was the first to see her coming. His eyes grew wide, the nostrils in his displaced nose flared, and his face turned even paler as he looked over my shoulder.

"Caly," he said, not as a greeting to her but as a warning to me. Then, without so much as an "Excuse me," he disappeared.

"Who you talking to?" Caly asked.

"What? Oh . . . I," I noticed my phone on the table. "My mom. It was on speakerphone."

"Oh," she said before sitting down next to me inside her cheerleading uniform. She sat with her back against the fold-up, cafeteria-style table, crossed her legs, folded her arms, and faced the others. "I just wanted to tell you that ..."

Before she could finish, Terwilliger arrived and interrupted her. He extended his hand to Caly. "Let's go," he said.

"Pete's giving me a ride home," she explained. "I'm still grounded and I'm on his way." She took Terwilliger's hand and allowed him to pull her to her feet. "Goodbye, T.J." she said, and they walked away.

"Always my ass," I said inaudibly, having lost all hope.

As they reached the door, a good ten yards from where I was sitting, I rose abruptly and called, "Hey, Pete." The sounds of forks and spoons and conversation stopped. Every set of eyes trained themselves on an apparent showdown. Even the coaches' table fell silent and attentive. Coach Harris stood up just in case. For what seemed like minutes but was only seconds, my eyes ping-ponged back and forth from Caly to Terwilliger.

"Good Luck," I finally said.

Terwilliger paused, looked around, gave a backwards nod, then slipped out the door with Caly in tow.

I sat down. The balloon of tension deflated, and the volume began its climb back to rock concert levels.

Moose returned. "Fuck him, man. He's a dick," he said then changed the subject. "You ready for tonight?"

"Not much to be ready for. There's no way Harris will put me in. He'll stick some sophomore in there to hand off to Morrison before he calls my number. But, if by some miracle it happens, remember, you told me that you'd always have my back."

"I'm not sure that extended into eternity, but you got it, brother," Moose said in his best Hulk Hogan voice then disappeared.

Chapter Nineteen

Friday Evening, All Souls Day, November 2, 201_

The atmosphere and noise level in the Ducks' locker room was the exact opposite of the VFW. The tension was thick as my teammates progressed methodically through pregame rituals and superstitions, each with ear buds hanging from their ears or headphones over the top of them. The intensity of playoff football was exponentially more amplified than for a regular season game, and it would only increase with each win. I sat in front of my locker in my black, padded game pants and a t-shirt, watching the others from a dispassionate distance.

This was the first game in over a season and a half that I wouldn't be the starting quarterback. I missed tight-roping the edge between utter terror and exhilaration. However, with no chance of getting into the game, my nerves and excitement remained in check.

Knowing that I had been relegated to carrying a clipboard, none of my teammates bothered to visit me at my locker or to slap me the occasional, relevant-to-nothing high-five. During position meetings, Coach McKuen directed all of his questions and instructions to Terwilliger, who struggled to maintain his bravado. During pregame warm-ups, my attention was continually drawn to the sidelines and stands in search of Coach Markinson. I watched my parents take their usual position in the top row of the general admission bleachers beneath the press box and several sections apart from where the Stones' sat in their cushioned and backed reserved seats.

A half hour prior to kick-off, the players from both teams relinquished the field and returned to their respective locker rooms for final instructions, reminders, and pep talks. The aluminum bleachers on both sides were crammed so full that a three-deep ring of spectators was forced to stand behind the interior, waist-high, chain-link fence that surrounded the field. Late arrivals were being turned away at the gate by the exasperated fire chief.

I was last in the line of Ducks as we funneled single-file into the single door of the locker room. I tuned in to the spectacle of high school football in a way I hadn't experienced it since I was in middle school and watching from the stands. I listened to the martial strains of the Ducks Marching Band as they stormed the field for their pregame show. I heard the individual exhortations of random, faceless voices in the crowd extolling my teammates to "Kick Ass!" The smell of French fries and popcorn filled my nostrils and triggered hunger pangs in my empty stomach, which was usually full of undigested nerves at this point on game night.

A northeast wind had blown off the clouds of the day and left behind a crisp, cool night beneath one of the blackest skies I had ever seen. While I waited for the jam to unclog, I removed my helmet, tilted my head back, and looked up through the rising fog of my own exhaled breath. The insanely-bright stadium lights obscured any hope I may have had of locating my place in the universe and of providing a realistic perspective to the significance of the events of the past week in any larger scheme of things – a "larger scheme" I'd all but given up on.

"T.J. Farrell," an unfamiliar voice stated not as a question but as a matter of fact and drew my attention down from the heavens. I looked into the face of Coach Markinson. He wore a navy blue letterman's-style jacket with leather sleeves and "Toledo Football" embroidered in gold on his left breast. "Coach Markinson," he added by way of unnecessary introduction. "Good luck tonight, son. I'm looking forward to watching you play."

"You're here?" I said befuddled. Clearly, he hadn't received the memo regarding my benching. Whatever scheme Dr. Stone and Coach Harris had cooked up, Coach Markinson was not yet in on it.

"Of course I am," he said. "I'm looking forward to watching you play."

I didn't say another word. I simply shook his hand and watched as he worked his way around my teammates to the locker room entrance, where he located Coach Harris. They were almost immediately joined by Dr. Stone, who must have been watching for him from his place in the stands. The three of them schmoozed like old fraternity buddies.

When I'd finally made my way into the locker room, everyone else was making last-minute uniform adjustments and trips to the toilet. When all of the coaches and players were ready and gathered in the locker room, Coach began his pep talk. "Gentlemen, this is a special night. However, all that we've accomplished in the regular season means nothing. It has only served to bring us to this point."

I had always listened intently to Coach's pep talks, not so much in search of inspiration or wisdom but because it helped to pass those excruciating minutes prior to kick-off. Looking around the locker room, I was surprised by how little attention the other players actually paid. Most of the starters were too engrossed in their own self-absorbed rituals, nervous tics, and visualizations of their assignments to pay much attention to Coach's bullshit. The underclassmen, who wouldn't play a down, seemed indifferent to the whole affair and would probably be just as happy with a loss and a reprieve from practicing another week.

Without Moose, I didn't even bother to listen to "Lose Yourself" or to write *Seize the Day* on my wrist tape.

"Many are called but few are chosen, the good book says," Coach continued. "*We* have been chosen, men. When this season began, hundreds of teams dreamed of playing tonight, but only thirty-two in the entire state of Ohio are left. However, the playoffs are sudden death. Lose tonight and it's all over. The season will have been a failure. I'd be lying – and you know it – if I said that anything short of a state championship is acceptable – to me, yourselves, your folks, or this town. This is *our* year. Your coaches have prepared; you have prepared. All that's left is to go out there and take it, and it begins tonight with Lakeview."

A few players testified: "C'mon!" "Let's Go!" "This is our house!"

"Play every down as if it's your last," Coach exhorted and locked eyes momentarily with me. "Because it may just be." After pausing for dramatic effect, Coach ordered us to take a knee. First, he lead us in the "Lord's Prayer," then with me hanging on the periphery, he commanded us to "bring it in." Everyone but me, gathered close around him in a huddle, and with their right hands, they reached for the center pole formed by Coach's own extended arm and hand. "One! Two! Three!" Coach called and the team answered, "Ducks!"

The circle disintegrated and the team began the slow process of reversing the slow entry we'd just completed of funneling into the locker room. I remained in the rear, so that after the penultimate Duck had exited, it left Coach Harris and I alone and staring disdainfully into one another's eyes. I made a move towards the door, but he stepped in front of me and blocked my way. "If it weren't a distraction that I don't need tonight, I'd collect your gear and remove you from this locker room so fast it would make your head spin."

I laughed at the notion of his "making my head spin." It hadn't *stopped* spinning for over a week.

"What's so funny?"

"Nothing, Coach. That's fine. You do what you think you've got to do. But I'm not quitting."

"You do understand that I will make sure that Coach Markinson walks out of here tonight with that scholarship still in his pocket?"

"Yes, sir. I suppose you're right about that."

"And you do understand that after I win my two hundredth game tonight and make this playoff run, it will be me, not you, who escapes this town?"

"Yes, sir. I suppose you're right about that too."

Having expected but not received blowback, Coach stared long and hard into my eyes before stepping to the side and allowing me to join my teammates just in time to join the rear of the Ducks' phalanx as it reformed in the end zone. After a Morrison-lead team break, we uncoiled, elongated, ran through the cheerleaders' paper hoop then came together once more, like a *Slinky*, to the sound of a tumultuous roar. On my way through the ring, Caly and I shared an extended gaze. Along the home sidelines, my teammates jumped up and down and slapped one another on their shoulder pads and helmets. To protect my aching head, I stayed to the fringe, where I found a football and offered Terwilliger to warm him up. He told me to "Fuck off."

Cory Morrison drove the home crowd into a frenzy when he returned the opening kick-off ninety-five yards for a score. "The rout is on," agreed the prematurely self-congratulating Ducks Nation. After Lakeview's first possession, a three-and-out, the Ducks' offense took the field without me. I glanced into the stands and read Coach Markinson's confusion and, I would suspect, irritation over having come to see me play only to watch me watch. We rode Morrison to a first-and-goal at the Lakeview nine yard-line, but Scags was flagged for holding and the drive stalled. Our kicker shanked the field goal attempt. After holding Lakeview on downs, our next series ended when, after a string of Morrison runs, Coach broke script and called for a play-action pass. Terwilliger put too much air under his throw, which allowed the free safety to pick it off in the end zone for a Lakeview touchback. I made sure to walk past Coach Harris after the interception, as if to remind him, "I'm still here if you need me to save your sorry ass."

The second quarter began with Morrison ripping off what appeared to be an amazing forty-five yard touchdown run. Beginning right on a simple toss sweep, he reversed field when he ran into a wall of would-be tacklers. Morrison turned towards his own goal line, surrendering ten additional yards in the process. A collective groan erupted from the home side bleachers in anticipation of a huge loss of yardage. The backside defensive end was in perfect position; however, all he could manage was to grab onto Morrison's right stiff-arm. The defensive end spun Morrison an entire revolution until the tackler was on his knees and the two looked like a pair of ice dancers. Cory landed on top of him but managed to keep both his knees and elbows from touching the turf. For just an instant, Lakeview's defenders quit the chase. But Morrison bounced off the tackler, juked a pursuing linebacker, then outraced the entire Lakeview defensive backfield down the left sidelines for an apparent score and a two touchdown advantage. The Ducks fans went berserk.

Like sirens in the distance, however, the grating sound of whistles broke through the celebration of Ducks players and fans. A referee, tracing Morrison's footsteps and repeatedly crossing his arms over his head, finally caught up to the play and retrieved the ball from a confused Morrison. While all watched in disbelief, the referee marched back downfield to the original line of scrimmage. He spotted the ball and held up two fingers to signal second down.

This time both sides of the stadium's bleachers went berserk.

The official had inadvertently blown his whistle at the spot where everyone, including him, assumed that Morrison would be tackled, but no one had heard the whistle. According to the rules, the down had to be re-played. Morrison spiked the football in anger and drew an unsportsmanlike conduct penalty. The end result was not only the loss of the touchdown but of an additional fifteen yards. Reeling from the sudden change of events, the Ducks' offense was unable to gather itself and punted the ball away three plays later.

The remainder of the half was played to a stalemate with no scoring threats generated by either team. The Ducks dominated the action; however, the score remained uncomfortably close. If the field had been eighty yards long rather than a hundred, it would have been a massacre, but each time the Ducks advanced into the red zone, they managed to screw it up and come away scoreless. The Ducks limped back to the locker room at halftime with a seven to nothing lead and an unexpected struggle on their hands.

With his goal of winning his two hundredth game in jeopardy and his team failing to impress Coach Markinson, Coach Harris tore into a chauvinistic rampage. "I've seen powder puff football games played more physically than I've seen out there tonight. You girls need to sprout some balls and trade your panties for some jock straps. You've got twenty-four minutes to set it right. You'd better play each of those minutes like they're your last. Because, if you don't, seniors, they very well may be. Now, let's go!"

Despite Coach's pleas and haranguing, the second half began identically to the first, except, this time, it was a Lakeview return man who took the opening kick-off to the house and knotted the score. A pall of silence, unlike any I could remember, fell over the home half of Ducks Stadium. The score was tied at seven, and the previously absurd notion that we might actually lose became plausible.

Lakeview, invigorated by finding themselves in a game that they couldn't have realistically expected to win, played inspired defense throughout the third quarter. The Ducks players, even the coaching staff, seemed to be playing not to lose rather than to win. During a timeout, I noticed that Dr. Stone and Coach Markinson had vacated their seats and were standing behind our sidelines and mirroring the movements of Coach Harris. I assumed that Coach Markinson had already given up on me and was attempting to get a read on Coach Harris's demeanor and game management skills.

Terwilliger's inexperience had resulted in very conservative play calling from Coach Harris. Once Lakeview figured that out, they began to load up near the line of scrimmage, positioning themselves to stop Morrison and daring us to throw with our virgin quarterback.

After another thwarted drive and a punt, I saw Coach McKuen pull Coach Harris aside. They engaged in a brief but heated conversation in which McKuen seemed to be pleading a case. I didn't have to hear it to know that it was about putting me in the game. Calls to "Put Farrell in" had been raining down from the stands in increasing frequency throughout the third quarter. Even through their headsets, the coaches had to be feeling the pressure caused by my benching. I didn't need to be a lip reader, however, to understand the emphatic "No!" with which Coach Harris ended the discussion.

Early in the fourth quarter, we caught a huge break when Lakeview's running back fumbled. Danny Sorenstam alertly picked up the live ball and returned it to the Lakeview four yard line before he was pushed out of bounds. Three hand-offs to Morrison and we were in the end zone. Based on the inefficiency of the Lakeview offense, the extra point seemed to put the game out of reach at fourteen to seven.

Coach ordered a squib kick on the ensuing kickoff that Lakeview recovered at its own forty yard line. With fewer than eight minutes remaining in the fourth quarter, they strategically reduced the contest to a ten-yard game. They buttoned up their offense by closing up their splits on the offensive line so that each lineman stood foot-to-foot. They replaced their wide-outs with tight ends, and they sent in a third running back as an additional lead blocker. Calling only basic, low risk/low reward running plays, Lakeview began to move the ball in two to five yard increments. Twice they went for the first down on fourth and short and got it. They were consistently moving the chains and keeping the drive and their impossible dream of victory alive.

It was a simple strategy: grind the clock and keep the ball out of the Ducks' and Cory Morrison's hands. Their hope was to tie the score in regulation then play to win in overtime. If that plan failed, however, they would be forced to surrender the ball on downs with little chance of getting it back with enough time to launch another drive.

During Lakeview's grinding march, Coach Harris used both of his remaining timeouts in order to slow Lakeview's rising momentum, to rest his defense, and to exhort his defenders to stiffen. But, the behemoth road grater into which the Lakeview offense had transformed itself continued to move methodically down the field. With under two minutes remaining in the game, Lakeview's tailback followed the tandem lead block of his backfield mates into the Ducks' end zone.

Lakeview chose not to go for the risky two point conversion and the win; instead, they sent out the extra point team. They would settle for the tie and take their chances in an overtime session. However, Morrison bulled his way through the center of the Lakeview line, blocked the kick, and preserved the Ducks' one point lead.

Lakeview failed in its onside kick attempt, so barring a miracle, the Ducks had won. Their faithful expelled a collective sigh of relief, and celebrations erupted throughout the stands and on the sidelines. The student section emptied the bleachers and stood waiting to jump the fence and to flood the field. The Ducks' band ripped through an ear-shattering medley of fight songs.

With only a single remaining timeout, Lakeview could only stop the clock one time. All we needed to do was run three "kneel downs" from the "Victory Formation" in which two halfbacks align next to the quarterback and a third "safety" back stands fifteen yards behind the quarterback, who, when he takes a direct snap from center, kneels immediately to stop the play.

Disappointed Lakeview fans filed from their bleachers and began heading for their cars. Few on the Ducks' side were even paying attention when, after the second snap, the Lakeview middle-linebacker dove headfirst over Scags and made direct helmet-to-helmet contact with Terwilliger, who was kneeling defenselessly and not expecting to be hit. Inexplicably, the officials failed to penalize the clear personal foul. Perhaps, they were hoping to expedite the play, end the game, and quell the mounting animosity between the two squads.

Woozy from the hit, Terwilliger rose to his feet and stumbled to the sidelines weaving like a drunk frat boy. I quickly scrawled *Seize the Day* on the tape over my wrist with the pen I'd been using to chart plays.

Because he was prematurely glad-handing Dr. Stone and Coach Markinson, Coach Harris failed to realize that he needed a quarterback to replace the injured Terwilliger. He must have nearly stroked-out when he returned his attention to the field and saw my number six entering the huddle. "Timeout! Timeout!" He repeatedly yelled to the side judge, but he had no timeouts left.

I could hear Coach Harris screaming to anyone who would listen, "What's Farrell doing out there? Who sent him in? Farrell! Farrell! Farrell!" He yelled to my selectively-deaf ears.

"Hey," Morrison said when he saw me approaching the huddle, "looks like the Goonies are coming in for mop up, boys. Oh, and sorry about you and your girlfriend."

"Shut up, Morrison, you asshole," Scags said.

Keeping my cool and focus, I called the play, "Victory formation, on one. Ready?"

"Break," the offense answered, with the exception of Morrison, who smugly retreated to his safety position.

I looked over my shoulder past Morrison and eyed the clock indifferently ticking off the game's final seconds. This would be the last play of the game, the season and most likely of my entire football career. The thought even crossed my mind that a solid hit to the head might just kill me. I didn't care.

In the middle of my cadence, I saw Coach Harris out of the corner of my eye. He was pointing his finger directly at me and screaming, "Don't you do it, son! Don't you do it!"

But it was too late.

I looked Coach Harris squarely in the eyes, called "Hut," and took the snap from Scags. Having already been warned by the referees against unnecessary roughness and prepared to concede the victory, the Lakeview defenders didn't even fire off the line. They merely watched in full anticipation of my taking the final knee and ending the game.

I, however, had something entirely different in mind.

Instead of going straight to my knee, I took the snap and, standing fully erect, calmly backed a few steps off the line of scrimmage.

Not having heard an immediate whistle, Scags turned around to see what was happening. When he saw the devilish gleam in my eyes, he said, "Don't do it, T.J. Take a knee, man."

"Take a knee, asshole!" Morrison threatened from behind.

Confused by the events, the Lakeview defenders took a tentative few steps toward me as my offensive linemen stepped between to block their way.

"Go down, T.J.!" Scags yelled as I took another step back.

Coach Harris was literally on the field nearly to the hash marks screaming at me to go to a knee. The side judge was forced to hold him back physically and to throw a flag for Coach's unsportsmanlike behavior, but the play continued.

The other officials looked at one another helplessly. They couldn't blow a whistle to end the game until a knee was downed. A simple genuflection would do.

I turned away from the line of scrimmage and faced our own end zone fifty yards away. Morrison stood in between. "Don't even try it, Farrell," he said through a shit-eating grin.

Like gunfighters in the streets of an Old West town, we each waited for the other to twitch.

I made a break. Morrison bore down on me, but in the millisecond before contact, either Morrison tripped or, I'd like to believe, Moose's ghost made a bone-crushing block that turned me loose on a dead sprint towards our own end zone with nineteen other players on my heels not sure whether to block or tackle and Coach Harris running along the sidelines screaming bloody murder the entire way.

I reached the one yard line, stopped, and turned to face my fast-closing pursuers, who drew to a halt ten yards away as if the football, which I held cocked in my right hand, was a suicide bomb. In a panoramic sweep, I looked into the faces of the players on the field and over their heads to Caly behind the bench, at my parents in the stands; at Dr. Stone and Coach Markinson with their jaws agape on the sidelines; at Coach Harris, fast-approaching in a maniacal rage; and at the citizens of Ducks Nation all with their hands pressed to the tops of their heads or to the sides of their faces. For a moment, I held them all hostage.

"It's not too late," I thought. "I can still take a knee right where I'm standing. 14 – 13, the Ducks win."

Suddenly, Morrison burst through the wall of players with a bead on me and prompted the remaining Ducks to follow his lead.

With no more time for internal debate, I spun, stepped into the end zone, and with my back turned away from my already-former teammates, I launched the tightest spiral of my career. The football whizzed out of my hand then passed through the uprights on a tightrope. The near officials threw their flags for intentional grounding then pressed their hands together above their heads to signal a safety and two points for Lakeview.

The scoreboard reluctantly registered the winning points for the Visitors, making the final score: Lakeview 15, Goodness Falls 14.

Morrison nailed me from behind nearly breaking me in half and bouncing my forehead violently off of the rock-hard turf. This time, I welcomed the pain that brought me back full circle to the very spot where my unraveling had begun exactly one week earlier.

He was followed by a flock of Ducks, who smothered me beneath the press of their bodies. If not for Scags peeling them off of me one-by-one, I might have died of suffocation.

I wouldn't have minded.

Once the realization of their victory sank in, the Lakeview players, coaches, and remaining fans broke into a frenzied celebration. The Ducks and their faithful froze as they were – lying, sitting, crouching, or standing – in a state of suspended animation.

"Are you crazy?" Scags asked.

"I've never felt so sane in my life,' I said or, at least, tried to say.

"What? I can't understand a word you're saying, man."

"I thed . . ." Before I could finish my slurred sentence, I fell back to the turf convulsing from a violent seizure. If not for the quick actions of Schultzie, I may have choked on my tongue and or vomit and died right there in the end zone. Of course, if not for the seizure, the Ducks fans may have lynched me from the goalpost. Same difference.

Again, I wouldn't have minded.

I was rushed unconscious to the hospital in Sandusky.

". . . and end low."

Epilogue

As I finish this, it's early morning. The night shift is surrendering to the day. The changeover is slow. The day shifters take their time, drink their coffee, settle in, and read the charts from the night before. It allows me ample opportunity to write without fear of interruption or discovery. I sit in a hospital recliner near the window and stare out through the double-panes. Snow is falling in quarter-sized flakes. The weathermen have been calling for eight-to-ten -inches. It's a Saturday in December, but it lacks that Saturday feeling. In this place, every day is pretty much like the one before it, except on Sundays when we're allowed visitors.

This place is Deer Park, a temporary facility for troubled youths. It literally sits in a park full of deer. Having found an island sanctuary in the midst of rural Erie County, the damn things are everywhere. The deer are supposed to be soothing to us residents, but in their glibness and arrogance, they act as if they own the place. In their comparative happiness, the deer are more of a source of annoyance than anything.

In better days, Deer Park had been an exclusive club. A fast-running trout stream, which only freezes during the coldest of Ohio winters, runs through the property. In the spring, summer, and fall, club anglers used to fly-fish from the banks in the solitary way of their art.

By the late nineties, however, the number of members willing to pay the high dues in exchange for communing with nature, reading a book from the well-stacked library, eating at the four-star quality dining room, or spending a night of rustic retreat in one of the upstairs suites had dwindled so low that board members had no choice but to disband and sell the clubhouse and property. When no serious buyer came forth – more out of spite than anything – they gifted the property to the county, which converted the site to its current identity as a treatment facility for adolescents suffering from mental illnesses, emotional disorders, and mild drug addictions. Based on those diagnoses, I guess, I'm what they'd call a triple threat. The residence hall, where I'm currently assigned, was the old clubhouse.

As I wrote at the beginning, I've been admitted for treatment of the CTE, Psychotic Major Depression, and as a suicide risk. The required referral was submitted by a University of Toledo Medical Center Psychiatrist, who'd been recommended by Dr. Stone. I'd been transferred there on the night of the game after I'd come to and freaked out in the emergency room of the hospital in Sandusky. By midnight, I was strapped to a hospital bed at UTMC and being guarded by two beefy security officers while I screamed bloody murder from the pain and either for medication or a bullet to the head.

To be honest, I don't remember much else of that evening – mostly the pain. That I remember. After reviewing my history of head injuries and conducting a battery of tests, including a PET scan, the doctors discovered I had a skull fracture and an acute subdural hematoma, or brain bleed. They were also the first to suspect the CTE. The fracture, which was over my left ear, most likely occurred on that last play of the last Friday of the regular season. The subdural hematoma began either at the same time or on the day Coach Harris inserted me as the Goon Squad quarterback. It was a slow bleed until Morrison tackled me in the end zone, at which time it became a gusher. The CTE, they figured, had been building up over countless blows to the head since I first started playing tackle football in the fourth grade.

Because of the rarity of someone so young contracting CTE and the even rarer chance discovery of it, my doctors are trying to arrange a transfer for me to Boston University, where, I've been told, they've been on the cutting edge of identifying CTE victims for years, and now, of establishing a protocol for treating its patients. But knowing the cause of pain doesn't make the pain go away, and I'm not too crazy about being the guinea pig for another set of eggheads. Besides, the dizziness sucks. The confusion sucks. The nonstop headaches suck. The meds, they suck too; they're sucking the me right out of me – at least what's left of me. And, there are no meds for lost souls or broken hearts.

I miss Caly.

By the time I'd arrived in Toledo in the early hours of Saturday morning, someone had already posted video of my final play on YouTube. On it, you can see Coach Harris chasing and screaming at me nearly the entire way. It's really quite comical. By Saturday evening, I had become an Internet sensation with over a hundred thousand hits in less than twenty-four hours. The "Wrong Way Quarterback" is what they'd labeled the video. By Sunday evening, the smart-ass "personalities" on ESPN had named my chase scene with Coach Harris one of the "Not Top Ten Plays of the Week." Over the top of the video, they'd dubbed the music to that "chicken dance" song that is always played at weddings.

Toledo called my parents and informed them that they were no longer interested in offering me a scholarship, nor was anyone else – not even "division three liberal arts schools in Iowa." I took some satisfaction in knowing that, after his tirade, Toledo was no longer interested in adding Coach Harris to their program either. Although officially still enrolled, not a single representative from Goodness Falls High School came to see me. I'm being tutored on premises and completing an online program with the intention of earning my diploma in June - whatever.

I haven't seen nor heard from Caly since that night, but we're not allowed cell phones, they screen my mail, and only my immediate family has been given visitation rights. Dr. Young says he's afraid Caly – or any of the Stones – may still be a "trigger" for me and it wouldn't be wise to see her just yet. I wrote a long confessional letter to Chief Johnson, but I somehow don't think it ever made it past Dr. Young's office much less to the post office. Besides, I doubt if the Chief would have or a court could have taken it as credible anyway. The testimony of a brain damaged, drug addled, story-switching witness isn't exactly airtight. However, I still hold on to the hope that, as Mr. Mortis, Chief Johnson, and Shakespeare all once asserted, "the truth will out." But I'm not holding my breath.

My mom visits on Sundays, but she's in complete denial and believes it has all been one big misunderstanding that will somehow work itself out. Despite the lack of significant progress in my condition over the six-plus weeks of my stay, I'm being released today. The cost of my room, board, and treatment and the lack of public aid has left my parents no alternative. Of course, if the Boston thing works out, they'll ship me out there. I'm sure those doctors can't wait to get their hands on my brain, dead or alive, and if they're willing to write off the cost of my care, what the hell?

An unexpected warning knock on the open door startles me and brings me to my feet. The wing I'm on is all boys. With good reason, therefore, the female nurses are petrified of walking in on us playing with ourselves at any and all hours of the day, but the mornings are especially dicey, so they usually give a warning knock. Before the nurse enters, I turn my back and stuff my notebook down my pants, which, of course, makes it look like I *have* been playing with myself.

"Good morning, T.J." she says in half-apology for interrupting me and with obviously false enthusiasm. Her voice sounds eerily familiar but not from the hospital – youthful yet not.

I remain with my back turned, willing to allow her the illusion that I'm hiding morning wood rather than my notebook.

"Dr. Young took ill unexpectedly and will be unable to see you today."

I don't respond. I rarely do.

"But," the nurse continues, "a visiting resident has arrived this morning and will be seeing to Dr. Young's patients until his return. He says that he has been in contact with Dr. Young and that he has been given permission to take care of your release. In fact, here he is. T.J. Farrell, this is Dr. . . . ."

A familiar man's voice intervenes, "Mortis."

I smile.

CPSIA information can be obtained at www.ICGtesting.com
Printed in the USA
LVOW12s1118030614

388402LV00010B/126/P